가난한 시인이 된 의사

최 윤 근 시 집

자화상

한때는 어항 속의 금붕어가 나의 자화상이었다
가을 찬바람에 흔들리는 외로운 코스모스였다가
때로는 추수 후 논두렁에 비 맞으며 서 있는
허수아비가 나의 자화상이었다

웃는 얼굴인가
우는 얼굴인가
찡그린 얼굴인가

문학청년이었다가
의사로 일생을 살다가
노인이 되어 시인된 사람

가난했다가 부자였다가
다시 가난해진 사람

사랑을 받았다가 주었다가
다시 사랑을 받고 있는 사람

건강했다가 육십에 전립선암에 걸리고
칠십에 급성 골수 백혈병에 걸려
수술 후유증과 줄기세포 이식 부작용으로

죽음의 문턱에 몇 번 갔다가 살아 돌아온 사람

항상 내일 죽을 수도 있다고 생각하지만
기를 쓰고 살겠다고 애쓰는 사람
그런 사람 여기 있어요

살아서 숨 쉬고 있는 나는 누구일까
어떤 삶의 목표를 지향하며 살아왔나

가지고 갈 것도 놔두고 갈 것도 없는 내가
아직도 욕심을 부리고 있다

종착역이 가까워져 내릴 준비를 하고 있다
아무리 찾아보아도 챙겨 갈 것은
녹슨 청진기와 지팡이 그리고 쓰다만 시 한 편이다

이 시집에 삽입된 그림은 저자의 작품들이며
편집은 내 사위인 이재윤 선생의 도움을 받았고
영문 번역은 ChatGPT의 도움을 받아 완성하였습니다
이 시집을 출간하기까지 도움을 주신 분들께 감사드립니다

Self-Portrait

Once, a goldfish in a bowl was my self-portrait,

Then, a lonely cosmos swaying in the chill autumn wind,

And at times, I saw myself as the scarecrow

Standing in the harvested field, rain-soaked and still.

Was it a smiling face,

A weeping face,

Or a frowning face?

I was a young literary dreamer,

Lived my life as a doctor,

Then aged into a poet.

I was poor, then wealthy,

And now, poor once again.

I received love, gave love,

And once more, am receiving love.

I was healthy, but at sixty, had prostate cancer,

At seventy, acute leukemia.

Surviving surgeries and stem cell transplants,

I brushed close to death's door and returned.

Always mindful that tomorrow could be my last,
Yet here I am, striving to live each day.

Who am I, alive and breathing?
What purpose has guided my life's journey?

With nothing to take, and nothing to leave behind,
Yet still, I find myself clinging to desires.

Now, as the final station draws near, I prepare to disembark.
There's nothing to take along but a rusty stethoscope,
A cane, and a half-finished poem.

The drawings in this collection are my own,
And I owe thanks to my son-in-law, Mr. Jae-Yoon Lee, for his editorial assistance,
And to ChatGPT for helping with the English translation.
To all who supported the creation of this collection, I extend my gratitude.

백남준을 기리며

차례

시인의 말

제1부

너의 친구가 되고 싶은 이유

꿈 ———— 14

Dreams ———— 16

이런 가을 언제 오려나 ———— 18

When Will That Kind of Autumn Return? ———— 21

안나 카레니나 ———— 24

As I delve into Anna Karenina ———— 25

완행열차의 간이역 ———— 26

A Country Station on the Slow Train Line ———— 28

마지막 오 분 ———— 30

The Last Five Minutes ———— 32

신앙인 되기 ———— 34

Becoming a Believer ———— 36

시 쓰기 ———— 38

On Writing a Poem ———— 40

그림자 ———— 42

The Shadow ———— 43

겨울은 그렇게 찾아오더이다 ———— 44

Thus Came Winter ———— 46

넋 ———— 48

The Soul ———— 50

칠십이종심소욕불유구七十而從心所慾不踰矩 ———— 52

At Seventy, the Heart Follows Its Desire ———— 54

스스로 찾아라 ——— 56

Seek It Yourself ——— 57

너의 친구가 되고 싶은 이유 ——— 58

Why I Long to Be Your Friend ——— 61

제2부

세월은 그렇게 왔다 그렇게 가더이다

이 세상의 모든 여인에게 ——— 66

To All the Women of This World ——— 68

세월은 그렇게 왔다가 그렇게 가더이다 ——— 70

Thus Time Came and Thus It Passed ——— 72

무명 시절 ——— 74

The Time of Obscurity ——— 76

개 같은 인생 ——— 78

A Dog's Life ——— 80

우릴 가난케 하는 것 ——— 82

What Makes Us Poor ——— 84

Carpe diem(오늘을 잡아라) ——— 86

Carpe Diem ——— 87

당신을 알고부터 ——— 88

Since Knowing You ——— 90

가을은 어디에 숨어 있는가 ——— 92

Where Is Autumn Hidden? ——— 94

동행 ———— 96

Companionship ———— 98

느낍니다 ———— 100

I Feel It ———— 101

스티브 잡스처럼 생각하기 ———— 102

Thinking Like Steve Jobs ———— 104

스치고 지나온 것들 ———— 106

The Things That Passed Me By ———— 108

제3부

그런 친구 못 보셨나요

칠월의 어느 날 ———— 112

One Day in July ———— 114

방귀 소리 ———— 116

The Sound of a Fart ———— 118

지퍼 ———— 120

The Zipper ———— 121

구속된다 ———— 122

Bound ———— 123

세월이 흘러가네 ———— 124

Time Flows On ———— 126

칠월의 정경 ———— 128

A Scene in July ———— 130

내 것 ——— 132

Mine ——— 134

노인의 외로움 ——— 136

The Solitude of the Elder ——— 138

그런 친구 못 보셨나요 ——— 140

Have You Seen Such a Friend? ——— 142

잔소리 ——— 144

Chatter ——— 145

달라져야 한다 ——— 146

There Must Be Change ——— 147

친구의 방문 ——— 148

A Friend's Visit ——— 149

가야 할 길 ——— 150

The Road Ahead ——— 152

제4부

가난한 시인이 된 의사

가난한 시인이 된 의사 ——— 156

The Poor Poet Who Was Once a Doctor ——— 158

봄소식 ——— 160

The Tidings of Spring ——— 161

운명 ——— 162

Fate ——— 164

돈보다 귀한 것 ———— 166

What Is Worth More Than Money ———— 168

힘들 때 기댈 수 있는 사람 ———— 170

Someone to Lean on in Difficult Times ———— 172

고향 집의 겨울 정경 ———— 174

Winter at the Old Home ———— 175

백지의 점 하나 ———— 176

A Dot on a Blank Page ———— 178

어둠도 빛이 되더라 ———— 180

Even Darkness Becomes Light ———— 182

인내심 ———— 184

Endurance ———— 186

슬픔은 그렇게 시작되더이다 ———— 188

How Sadness Begins ———— 190

너의 친구가 되고 싶은 이유

우연과 인연 사이

꿈

앞 내에 개나리 피는 봄이 오면 언 땅에서
움트는 새싹처럼 꿈틀대는 생명의 꿈을 꾸고 싶다

가뭄과 장마
무더운 여름날
시원한 바람 함께 즐기고
소나기 오면 우산 속 동행하는 우리를 꿈꾸고 싶다

황금빛 벌판
코스모스 피는 가을의
푸른 하늘 아래
자유를 마음껏 누리는 꿈

눈보라 치는 추운 겨울에
따뜻한 차방에 연인과 차를 마시며
레이디 가가의 I always remember us this way*를
들으며 공감하는 꿈을 꾸고 싶다

좌절했을 때 희망을 보는 꿈
숨 막힐 것 같은 어두운 동굴 속에 비치는
한 줄기 빛 같은 그런 꿈을 꾸고 싶다

꿈 그 얼마나 가슴 설레는 말인가
꿈 그 얼마나 달콤한 미래인가
꿈을 꿀 수 있어 행복하다

고난 속에서도 꿈을 꿀 수 있었던 것은
믿음이 있었기 때문이었고
지금도 꿈을 꿈 수 있는 것은
그대가 내 곁에 있기 때문이다

이루지 못할 꿈은 안타깝지만
그래도 꿈을 꾸기 위해 단잠을 잔다

* 레이디 가가가 부른 노래의 제목이자 마지막 소절. 꿈과 좌절, 사랑과 이별을 애절하게
표현한 노래. "나 항상 우리를 그렇게 기억하리라".

Dreams

When spring unfurls its golden flags of forsythia,

And the thawing earth stirs with trembling buds,

I wish to dream of life awakening,

As shoots rise from the soil in quiet exultation.

In the drought and in the flood,

Under the sweltering blaze of summer's cruel sun,

I long to feel the cool breath of winds,

To share in that joy with you,

And when the sudden storm breaks,

Let us walk together beneath the sheltering arc of one umbrella.

Upon the golden paths of autumn,

Where the cosmos sways like whispers in the breeze,

Under the vast, endless blue sky,

I dream of freedom,

Of hearts unbound, soaring as high as birds.

In the harsh, howling snows of winter's depths,

Let us find refuge in a warm, dim-lit corner,

Sipping tea with hearts intertwined,

As Lady Gaga sings of love's bittersweet refrain—

And I dream of us, remembering, understanding, and feeling it all.

When despair comes like a shadow upon my days,

I dream of a glimmer—just one beam of light—

That slices through the darkest cave,

A hope that leads me to breathe again.

Oh, how the word "dream" stirs the soul!

How sweet the promise of a future unseen,

For I am happy because I can dream.

In trials, still I could dream,

For faith was my companion.

Now, even as I dream once more,

It is because you walk beside me.

Though not all dreams reach their end,

Still, with a quiet smile, I close my eyes—

For even in sleep, I chase the dream anew.

이런 가을 언제 오려나

바람이 차다
낙엽은 떨어져 땅에 뒹굴고
길가 포장마차 안에선
길손들 매운 떡볶이에
따끈한 어묵 국물 마시며 찬바람을 피하고 있다

지난여름은 너무 더워
가을은 정녕 오지 않을 것 같았는데
가을은 잠깐 머물다
곧 떠나려 한다

요즘 세상 돌아가는 게 이상하다
추울 땐 아주 춥고
더울 땐 아주 덥고
장마질 땐 넘쳐흐르게 비가 오고
가뭄 땐 들판의 곡식들 다 타들어 갈 때까지 가물고
이쪽에서 총소리 들리고
저쪽에서 지진 나고

전장에선 나쁜 놈들은 멀쩡하고
어린이들 노인들
무고한 시민들만 죽어간다 하고

세상에 말세가 온 건가

하늘은 푸르고
기러기 날아오고
벌판엔 코스모스 하늘거리고
곡간엔 추수한 곡물들로 꽉 차 있는 늦가을
식구들 모어 앉아 웃고 떠들며
웃으면 복이 와요
TV 시청하는
그런 가을 언제 다시 오려나

유방암 완치 판정을 받은 아내의 칠순 때는
유람선 타고 지중해 여행 가고

팔순 친구들 모여
지리산 완등한 후
구례 장터 맛집에서 축하 파티하고

우크라이나 수도 키이우에서 K팝 가수들 축제가 열리고
기독교 신자들 떼 지어 예루살렘 성지 방문하고
세계의 젊은이들 가자지구에서 집 지어주기 봉사하고

세계의 독재자들 비명횡사하여 억눌렸던 시민들 자유를 찾고
평양에도 가을이 오고
이곳저곳에 세워졌던 김 부자 동상들 땅에 떨어져 낙엽처럼 뒹굴고
어린 뚱보 독재자는 종적 없이 사라졌고
가난과 시련 속에 살았던 북한 인민들 춤추며 자유를 만끽하는
이런 가을 언제 오려나

투표는 하되 인공지능이 부도덕한 자를 가려내어
국민의 대표가 될 수 없게 하고
지도자를 존경하며 따르고
사업가들은 사업가대로 공정하게
노동자들은 노동자들대로 만족하며 땀 흘려 일하는 사회
그런 가을 빨리 왔으면 좋겠다

When Will That Kind of Autumn Return?

The wind cuts through me, cold and sharp.
Leaves fall, rolling on the earth,
Their flight a silent dance of farewell.

By the roadside, beneath the thin veil of a street vendor's tent,
Travelers seek warmth—
Spicy tteokbokki on their tongues,
And in their hands, a cup of hot broth.

They flee the wind, but it follows, always near.
The summer—too fierce, too endless—
Had me believing autumn might never come.

And now, it arrives only to slip away,
A fleeting guest, vanishing into the horizon.
These days, the world moves strangely,
As if untethered from the seasons of old.

The cold becomes a biting frost,
The heat, an unbearable fire.
Rain no longer nurtures but floods,
And when the earth dries, it does so until nothing remains.

On one side, the sound of war,
On the other, the earth shudders and quakes.
In battle, the wicked remain unscathed,
While children, the elders, the innocent fall.

Is this the age of ruin?
The end of days?
Yet still, the sky remains impossibly blue,
Geese rise, drawn by an unseen force,
Cosmos flowers sway, fragile yet enduring,
The fields, full from harvest,
And families gather in laughter—
Laugh, and Fortune Will Come.

Oh, when will such a tender autumn return?
When my wife, healed from her breast cancer,
Turns seventy,
We will sail the Mediterranean—
A sea vast and eternal, as if time itself could be paused.

When I am eighty,
My friends and I will climb the mountains,
Celebrate in the simple, humble joy
Of a feast at Gurye's market.

In Kyiv, K-pop echoes through the streets,
While believers gather at Jerusalem's ancient walls,
And youth from all lands rebuild homes in Gaza—
Their hands stitching hope into the very earth.

The tyrants fall, not by war,
But by the weight of their own darkness.
The oppressed, no longer silent, reclaim their voice,
And autumn, long-awaited, will touch even Pyongyang.

Statues crumble like leaves,
The winds of change scattering them into dust.
The young dictator, bloated with arrogance,
Vanishes, as if he were never more than a shadow.

And the people—those long burdened by famine and fear—
Will rise, and in their joy,
They will dance in the streets of their new world.

The ballot remains,
But the hand of AI will guide us,
Separating the corrupt from the worthy.
Leaders will be followed, not out of fear,
But out of respect, earned and deserved.

Businessmen will act with fairness,
And laborers, with pride in their sweat,
Will find joy in their toil.
Such an autumn, I wish,
Will come soon,
So soon.

안나 카레니나

안나 카레니나를 읽으며
인간의 본능과 지혜에 대하여 생각해 본다

방종한 사랑도 사랑일까
강요된 인내심도 용서함일까

인간의 규범과 질서가 마구 피어나는
들판의 풀꽃을 간섭할 수 있을까

너의 사랑이 진실하다고 항변할 수 있으나
타인에게 슬픔을 주는 사랑은 은혜를 받을 수 없다

자연은 순리대로
봄에는 봄에 피는 꽃이 피어야 한다

사랑했는데
사랑에 대하여 왜냐고 묻고 있다

As I delve into Anna Karenina

I ponder the nature of human instinct and wisdom.

Is a reckless love still love?
Is forced patience a form of forgiveness?

Can the rules of man and order
intervene in the wildflowers blooming in the field?

You may argue that your love is true,
but a love that brings sorrow to others
cannot receive grace in return.

Nature unfolds in its own way;
in spring, the blossoms must bloom as spring dictates.

I loved, yet I find myself questioning:
Why, oh why, this enigma of love?

완행열차의 간이역

바흐의 G선상의 아리아는
느린 선율에도 가슴을 울린다

완행열차가 느리다고 예정 시간에
늦게 도착하는 것은 아니다

하루에 한 번 둘러 두세 명 타고 내리는
읍내의 작은 역은 한가롭기만 하다

십 년 전에도 그랬고 지금도 그렇다
나이 많은 역장이 기차가 들어올 때 한번 떠날 때 한번
깃발을 흔들면 그의 임무는 끝이다

모든 게 변한다
마을은 쇠락해 갔고
간절했던 것들이 무덤덤해졌다

기다리는 마음만큼 느리게
그리움을 채우기에는 이 완행열차가 제격이다

간이역엔 배웅하는 사람도 없고 석양만 외로이 비치고 있다
이 기차가 마지막 열차일지도 모른다

여기까지 느리게 왔으니
볼 것 다 보고
할 것 다 하면서 느리게 가면 되겠지

A Country Station on the Slow Train Line

Even Bach's Air on the G String,

Though slow in its flow, stirs the soul,

Much like the steady, measured journey of this slow train.

Yet, though the pace is languid,

It arrives just as the clock foretells.

A small station, where once a day

Perhaps two or three souls step off or climb aboard,

Lies quiet, unbothered by time's passage.

It was so ten years ago,

And so it remains.

The aging stationmaster,

His duties reduced to a wave of his flag,

Once when the train pulls in,

And once more as it pulls away—

His task is done.

All things change,

The village fades into forgetfulness,

And those longed-for moments once so vital,

Now seem distant, like whispers of a past life.

The waiting heart, too, slows—
And perhaps it is this slow train
That fills the gaps of longing just right,
Matching the pace of yearning.

No one is left to bid farewell at this station;
Only the sunset,
Lingers in lonely beams,
As if this train may be the last.

But having traveled this far at such a slow pace,
What more is there to rush for?
Now, with all that has been seen,
All that was to be done, done,
Perhaps it is best to keep moving slowly,
Until there is no more need to move at all.

마지막 오 분

사형 집행 전 오 분의 시간이 주어졌을 때
도스토옙스키는 아마도 자신의 양심과 마주했을 것이다

죽기 전 오 분은 너무나 짧은 시간이고 너무나 귀중한 시간이다
명예나 억만금의 재산이 무슨 소용이 있으랴
후회하기도 과거를 회상하기도 턱없이 짧은 시간이다

죽기 전 오 분이 주어진다면
나에게 상처를 준 자를 용서하고
내가 상처를 입힌 사람에게 용서를 구하며
마지막 오 분을 준 신에게
감사하며 평안한 마음으로 죽음을 맞이하겠다

도스토옙스키는 오 분의 시간이 지난 후
사형 집행은 취소되고 자유의 몸이 되었다

매일 마지막 오 분이라 생각하며
사랑하고
용서하고
오 분간 참회하고
오 분간 기도하고
오 분간 감사하면

영원한 자유인이 되지 않을까요

하루에 오 분간만 당신을 사랑할게요
하루에 오 분간만 당신을 그리워할게요
나의 오 분이 내 인생의 크기랍니다

The Last Five Minutes

Given five minutes before the sentence falls,

Dostoevsky, surely, stood before the mirror of his soul,

The time so brief, so precious—

What is the weight of honor, or the vastness of wealth,

In the face of such final moments?

Too short to linger in regret,

Too fleeting to grasp the past.

If five minutes were given to me before death,

I would forgive those who wounded me,

Seek the pardon of those I have wronged,

And with a heart unburdened,

Offer my final gratitude to the God

Who grants me these last breaths.

When the five minutes had passed,

Dostoevsky's chains were broken,

The execution called off,

And he walked free again.

What if we lived, each day, as though it were the final five minutes?

Loving in those five minutes,

Forgiving in those five minutes,

Repenting for five minutes,

Praying for five minutes,

Giving thanks for five minutes—

Could we not, then, become eternal,

Free of all chains?

For five minutes each day,

I will love you.

For five minutes each day,

I will long for you.

And in those five minutes,

The breadth of my life is held,

In its fullest expanse.

신앙인 되기

그와 나는 좋은 관계가 아니다
그와 만난 적도 없고
지은 죄가 없는데 그가 내 죄를 대속하여
십자가에 못 박혀 죽임을 당하셨단다

그것도 이천 년 전의 일을 믿고 따라오란다
물을 포도주로 만들고
오병이어의 기적
죽은 지 사흘 만에 부활하심을 믿으라 한다
나는 못 믿겠는데
키르케고르가 말했던가
패러독스를 믿어야 신앙인이 될 수 있다는 것을

나는 그와 그의 제자들이 남긴 언행을
대충 보고 대충 읽고 대충 행하며 냉담했다
거부하지는 않았지만
쉽게 받아들이지도 않았다

가끔 이런 생각은 해 보았다
시대를 초월해서 많은 사람들이
나보다 현명하고 훌륭한 사람들이 믿고 의지했던 신앙을
왜 나는 가까이 다가가지 못할까

죽음의 병상에서 하나님 도와주세요 살려주세요
이런 말이 선뜻 나오지 않았다
내가 너무 오랫동안 그를 등지고 살았으니
그의 이름을 부르기가 부끄러웠다

그의 이름을 부르고 그의 품에 안겨
기도하는 모습은 아름답다
자기 죄를 고백하고 가족을 위하여 이웃을 위하여
기도하는 이의 모습은 더욱 아름답다

나도 언젠간 그의 품에 안겨
나를 위하여 가족을 위하여
이웃과 나라를 위하여 기도할 수 있는
신앙인이 되기를 기원해 본다

Becoming a Believer

He and I are not well acquainted,
I've never met Him,
Nor have I committed a crime worthy of His notice.
And yet, they say He bore my sins,
Nailed to the cross,
Dying in my place.

They ask me to believe in this—
In an event two thousand years ago.
To believe He turned water into wine,
That He fed five thousand with a few loaves and fish,
That He rose from death after three days.
But I cannot.
Was it not Kierkegaard who said,
Only by believing the paradox can one have faith?

I have skimmed through His words,
Glanced over the deeds of His disciples,
Practiced half-heartedly,
Neither rejecting nor fully embracing.
My heart remained distant,
Neither cold nor warm.

Sometimes I wonder—
If across the ages,

So many, far wiser and nobler than I,
Have found solace and strength in this faith,
Why can't I draw nearer?

Even on the sickbed,
When others might call, "God, save me,"
The words stayed stuck in my throat.
Too long I had turned my back,
Too ashamed was I to speak His name.

Yet, the sight of those who do—
Who call His name,
And rest in His embrace,
Their prayers like songs of beauty—
Confessing sins,
Praying for family, for neighbors,
It is a sight too beautiful to ignore.

I hope, one day,
I, too, will rest in His arms,
Praying for myself,
For my family,
For my neighbors and my country—
I hope, one day,
I will become a believer.

시 쓰기

여백 속에 단어들이 병렬한다
감정들이 부딪히고 갈등한다
작은 불씨들이 장작처럼 타올라 시커먼 재가 된다

배고픔으로 목마름으로 언어들을 마셔보지만
만성 변비 환자가 되어 고통 속에 살기도 한다

윤동주처럼 우물 속에 갇혀 있는
자아를 안타까워하기도 하고

악마의 유혹에 넘어가
젊음은 얻었지만 순결한 마르가리타를 짓밟는
파우스트 박사가 돼보기도 하고

햄릿처럼 삶과 죽음을 고뇌해 보기도 하는
젊은 시인이여

시는 자유로운 영혼이다
파랑새처럼 하늘을 날고
꽃처럼 향기로워 관심을 모으지만
하루도 못 견디고 시든 꽃잎 되어
바람에 날리는 안타까움이여

젊은 시인이여 여백을 다 채우려 하지 말라
여백이 스스로 진실을 말할 때 독자들은 감동한다

On Writing a Poem

Words, like leaves in a gentle breeze, align,

And yet, within, emotions crash and strain,

As kindling does, they spark, ignite,

Until all that remains is ash upon the ground.

I thirst for words, and hunger for their taste,

Yet oft I find myself, as one who waits—

A sufferer of some great, unseen weight,

Burdened with thoughts that cannot yet be freed.

I, like Yun Dong-ju, gaze into the well,

And mourn the self, imprisoned in its depths.

Or like Faust, I yield to tempting youth,

But crush the innocent beneath my stride.

And as Hamlet, I ponder life and death,

A poet caught between the fleeting and the vast.

Such is the plight of the young poet's heart.

But poetry, like the wind, is free,

Like birds that soar across a boundless sky,

Or flowers that bloom, though brief their time,

To offer sweetness to a fleeting eye.

O young poet, seek not to fill each line,
For in the empty space, the truth may lie.
When silence speaks, the reader's soul is stirred,
More deeply than by any spoken word.

그림자

그림자 속에는 과거의 애련도
미래의 꿈도 들어 있지 않았네

내가 가까이 가면 그도 가까이 왔고
내가 멀어지면 그도 멀어져갔네

나무 그늘에 들어서면
그의 그림자도 나의 그림자도
나무 그림자에 묻혀 버렸다

뭉게구름의 그림자는 여기저기 흐르는데
낮엔 태양의 그림자는 자취가 없고
밤엔 달과 별의 그림자가 보이질 않네

그림자에는 세월이 흐른 흔적도 보이지 않고
풍상에 거칠어진 주름과 흰머리도 보이지 않네

우린 서로의 그림자를 밟으려 하지 않았네
그의 그림자가 더 크고 빛나기를 바라면서

그의 그림자와 나의 그림자가 하나가 될 때
그 속에서 쿵쿵 뛰는 사랑의 심장 소리가 들리기를 바랐네

The Shadow

In shadows, no trace of past sorrow lies,
Nor dreams of the future's hopeful skies.
When I drew near, so did it come close,
When I withdrew, it faded like a ghost.

Beneath the tree, where shadows rest,
My own and his together pressed,
Blended within the branches' shade,
As though in nature's grasp, they stayed.

Cloud shadows drift across the earth,
While the sun at noon leaves none at birth,
And by night, no moon nor stars on high
Cast shadows for my searching eye.

The shadow shows no mark of years,
No lines of care, no silvered hairs.
Yet we did not tread upon each other's shade,
Each hoping the other's light would never fade.

When his shadow and mine as one became,
I wished to hear love's beating heart the same,
For in that union, in shadows deep,
Our love's true pulse might forever leap.

겨울은 그렇게 찾아오더이다

겨울은 신혼집에 불쑥불쑥 찾아오는
시누이처럼 그렇게 심술궂게 찾아오더이다

북풍한설에 코스모스 꽃잎 휘날리며
냉정한 모습으로 그렇게 찾아오더이다

낙엽은 떨어져 뒹굴고 앙상한 나뭇가지의
초라한 모습으로 그렇게 찾아오더이다

동짓달 긴 밤
잠 못 들어 하며 닥쳐올 시런 걱정하는 사이
그 걱정 틈새에 끼어 슬며시 찾아오더이다

철새는 떠나가고
높은 하늘에 북쪽에서 날아오는 기러기 떼에
묻혀 그렇게 겨울은 찾아오더이다

쌀 곳간이 채워지고
김장 김치 담가놓고
연탄이 쌓이면
겨울은 감사 기도처럼 그렇게 찾아오더이다

지구촌의 어디에선가
초대받지 않은 침략자들에 의해 도시는 파괴되고
죄 없는 군인과 양민들이 죽어가는 겨울
추위를 쫓아낼 태양처럼
평화의 바람도 그렇게 찾아오더이다

끝나지 않을 것 같은 모진 겨울도 그렇게 찾아왔다가
따뜻한 봄이 되니 꽃망울을 남기고 바쁘게 떠나더이다

Thus Came Winter

Winter arrived, unannounced,
Like a sister-in-law, storming in uninvited,
Her presence cold, unkind,
As north winds scattered the cosmos petals—
So winter came, in all her chilling pride.

Leaves fell and tumbled to the ground,
Bare branches stood in shivering grace,
A desolate sight, unwelcomed,
Yet still, winter came with steady pace.

In the long night of winter's reign,
Sleepless, I feared the trials to come,
And in those cracks of worry,
Winter slid silently, her work begun.

The migratory birds flew south,
And in their place, the geese from the north,
Trailing the high winds,
So winter followed, and found her way.

But when the granaries filled with rice,

And jars of kimchi stood ready for the frost,

When charcoal was stacked high with care,

Winter came softly,

Like a prayer of gratitude whispered in the cold air.

Yet somewhere on this earth,

In lands ravaged by unbidden wars,

Where cities fall to invaders' hands,

And the innocent lie beneath the snow,

May peace, like the sun that warms the land,

Come as winter leaves,

And drive away the cold.

For even the harshest winter,

Though long and bitter,

Gives way to spring's warm embrace,

Leaving buds of hope behind—

And thus, winter departs in quiet haste.

넋

향촉의 연기 속에 넋이 있는가
무녀의 희고 긴 소매 속에 넋이 있는가

흘러가는 구름 속엔
스치는 저 바람 속엔 넋이 담겨 있을까

넋이 맑게 채워져야
산이 산대로 보이고
물이 물대로 보이고
사람이 사람대로 보일 거다

오만이 끼어 있지 않아야
거짓이 끼어 있지 않아야
미움이 끼어 있지 않아야
맑고 깨끗한 넋을
유지할 수 있다

꽃처럼 아름다운 넋
바람처럼 자유스러운 넋
태양처럼 빛나는 넋이
우리를 구원한다

못된 짓을 하면 넋이 나가고
어처구니없는 짓을 하면 넋이 빠진다

갈매기의 눈에는 파도치는 바다의 넋이 담겨 있고
기러기의 눈에는 북쪽 추운 툰드라의 넋이 담겨 있겠지

꽃밭에서 꽃의 아름다움에 취해
꽃향기에 취해 넋이 나가고
호숫가에선 일렁이는 잔물결에 넋을 뺏긴다

작은 선행을 하고 늘 감사하는 사람은 작은 선행이 쌓여
세상을 따뜻하게 하는 넋을 갖게 되겠지

당신이 넋이 나가 있을 때 슬며시 다가가
내 사랑이 담긴 넋으로 너를 채워주리라

The Soul

Does the soul dwell within the rising incense?

Or perhaps within the long, flowing sleeves of the shaman?

Might it drift upon the passing clouds,

Or slip by in the whispering wind?

Only when the soul is clear,

Can the mountains reveal themselves as mountains,

The waters as waters,

And people as they truly are.

The soul must remain untainted—

Free from pride,

Free from lies,

Free from hatred.

Only then can it remain

Pure and bright.

A soul as beautiful as a flower,

As free as the wind,

As radiant as the sun—

Such a soul shall redeem us.

If one acts with malice, the soul departs,
If one acts foolishly, the soul is lost.

In the eye of the seagull,
The soul of the restless sea is reflected,
And in the eye of the wild goose,
The cold tundra of the north is carried.

In the garden, drunk on the beauty of flowers,
Lost in the fragrance, the soul slips away,
And by the lake, the gentle ripples steal it.

One who performs small deeds of kindness,
And lives in constant gratitude,
Will find their soul growing,
Warming the world with its light.

And when your soul is lost in distraction,
I will come to you quietly,
Filling you with my love,
To restore your soul once more.

칠십이종심소욕불유구 七十而從心所慾不踰矩*

하늘을 나는 새처럼 자유스러워지고 싶고
따뜻한 아랫목에 같이 늙어가는 부인과
마주 앉아 파전에 막걸리 한 잔 걸치고 싶고

툇마루에 홀로 앉아 노을 진 석양을 바라보며 시 한 수 쓰고 싶고
문득 생각나 손주들 선물 사가지고 딸네 집 들르고 싶고

일주일이 토요일과 일요일로 채워진 친구들과
땀 흘리며 청계산 등반도 하고 싶고

인간만사 새옹지마
힘든 친구 잘된 친구들 만나
옛이야기 나누어 보고 싶기도 하고

재래시장에 들러 해장국에 소주 한 잔 마시며
주모와 세상사 이야기도 해보고 싶다

미련을 남긴 과거
꿈이 없는 내일을 탓하며 신세 한탄도 해보고

칠십 이상의 생활은 바람이 불면 바람이 부는 데로
눈서리 내리면 눈서리 맞으며

걸어온 길 또 걷고

만난 사람 또 만나고

실수했던 일 또 실수하며

생각 놓고 세월을 보내는 것이다

* 칠십이 되면 마음에 하고자 하는 바를 그대로 따라도 법도에 벗어나지 않는다. ─공자

At Seventy, the Heart Follows Its Desire

I long to be free, like a bird soaring high,

To sit with my aging wife,

In the warmth of our hearth,

Sharing a simple meal of pancake and rice wine.

I wish to sit alone on the wooden porch,

Watching the sun set,

Writing verses in the fading light.

Or, on a whim,

Visit my daughter's home, bearing gifts for my grandchildren.

Saturdays and Sundays stretch endlessly—

Friends gather,

We hike the trails of Cheonggye Mountain,

Our bodies glistening with the sweat of effort and joy.

Life is a wheel, ever turning,

Meeting friends,

Some who have struggled,

Some who have thrived—

Together we share stories of days long past.

I wish to wander through the market,

Savor a bowl of soup,

Raise a glass of soju,

And talk with the tavern keeper

Of life's unending flow.

Sometimes, I find myself lamenting—

The past, with its lingering regrets,

And tomorrow, which seems to hold no dreams,

And in these moments, I mourn.

But at seventy, life becomes the wind's whisper—

When the wind blows, I go with it,

When the frost descends, I feel its touch.

I walk the path I have walked before,

Meet those I have met before,

Make the same mistakes again and again,

And in this repetition, I let go of thought,

And let time carry me forward.

스스로 찾아라

대도시 뒷골목에서 배고파 하고
돌아서 갈까 망설여 보기도 하고
이름 모를 해변에서는 바위에 부딪히는
파도를 보며 흘러가 버린 세월을 생각했다

가다 보면 이정표가 나타난다

뉴욕 걸어서 사만 리
에덴의 동쪽 걸어서 삼만 리
스틱스강* 걸어서 육 개월
석양이 지는 언덕 걸어서 이틀

내가 온 길은 어둠에 묻혀 있고
내가 갈 길은 안개에 젖어 있다
어디로 갈까
스스로 길을 찾아야 한다
팀셜**

* 스틱스강 저승에 이르는 강.
** 구약성서 창세기 4장 6절. 스스로 선과 악을 다스려라.
스스로 찾아라.
존 스타인벡
에덴의 동쪽

Seek It Yourself

In the alleyways of the great city, I hunger,

Pausing, unsure if I should turn back.

On a nameless shore, watching the waves crash against the rocks,

I think of the years that have slipped away with the tide.

Yet, as I walk, signposts emerge.

"To New York, forty thousand miles on foot,"

"To the east of Eden, thirty thousand miles to walk,"

"To the River Styx, six months of journey,"

"To the hill where the sun sets, just two days more."

The road behind me is buried in shadow,

And the path ahead is veiled in mist.

Where should I go?

I must seek the way myself.

Timshel.*

* The River Styx: The river leading to the underworld.
* Timshel: "Thou mayest"—a choice given in the Old Testament, Genesis 4:6, to rule over sin.
Seek it yourself.
John Steinbeck, East of Eden.

너의 친구가 되고 싶은 이유

내가 너의 친구가 되고 싶은 이유는
옳고 그름에서 옳음을 추구하고
선과 악에서 선의 편에 섰기 때문이다

내가 너의 친구가 되고 싶은 이유는
네가 완벽한 사람이 아니기 때문이다
때로는 돌부리에 걸려 넘어지기도 하고
유혹에 넘어가 손해 보기도 하고
감정을 다스리지 못하고 화를 내는 평범한 사람이기 때문이다

내가 너의 친구가 되고 싶은 이유는
너의 가정이 행복하기 때문이다
네가 부자도 아니고 성공한 것도 아닌데
네 구실을 알고 책임과 의무를 다하고
가족들에게 사랑을 주고 존경을 받기 때문이다

내가 너의 친구가 되고 싶은 이유는
네가 앞산의 진달래
뒷동산의 홍매화
들판의 개망초를 예뻐하고
맑고 푸른 하늘을 보며 감탄하고
욕심부리지 않고 사는 태도 때문이다

내가 너의 친구가 되고 싶은 이유는
겉과 속이 다르지 않고
거짓 없이 진실하기 때문이다

내가 너의 친구가 되고 싶은 이유는
항상 웃고 긍정적이며
본인에게는 엄격하고
타인에게는 관대하고
스스로 겸손하기 때문이다

내가 너의 친구가 되고 싶은 이유는
네가 머리가 좋고 천재적인 재능이 있어서가 아니라
항상 노력하고 실패해도 포기하지 않기 때문이다

내가 너의 친구가 되고 싶은 이유는
네가 부자라서가 아니라
작은 것에 만족하고 감사하며
이웃을 배려하기 때문이다

내가 너의 친구가 되고 싶은 이유는
네가 성인군자가 아니라

자기 잘못을 인정하고
용서를 빌고
잘못을 시정하려는 태도 때문이다

나도 그런 친구가 될 수 있을까
부끄럽지 않은 너의 친구가 되고 싶다

Why I Long to Be Your Friend

I wish to be your friend,
For you stand where the righteous dwell,
And seek the path where goodness leads,
Not lost in falsehood's tangled spell.

I wish to be your friend,
Not for some perfect grace you hold,
But for the stumbles on your way,
The moments where, like autumn leaves,
You fall and rise again each day.

You are not above the pull of life,
The tempests of temptation's sway,
But still you stand, an honest soul,
Unmoved by pride or fleeting gain.

I wish to be your friend,
For in your home the hearth is warm,
Not with riches or grandeur spread,
But with love that fills each room,
Where duty is a guiding thread.

I wish to be your friend,

For you see beauty in the hills,

In the azalea's tender bloom,

In plum trees swaying in the breeze,

And wildflowers' quiet perfume.

You look to skies of endless blue,

And marvel at their simple grace,

Without desire to hoard or claim,

But find contentment in this place.

I wish to be your friend,

For your heart, both pure and true,

Holds no disguise or hidden face,

Your words reflect the inner you.

I wish to be your friend,

For kindness rests upon your smile,

And though you hold yourself with care,

Your mercy makes your heart worthwhile.

Not for wisdom sharp or grand,

But for the way you strive and stand—
Even when the world conspires,
You rise again, with soul afire.

I wish to be your friend,
Not for wealth or worldly things,
But for the joy you find in small,
The grace with which your spirit sings,
And cares for others, one and all.

I wish to be your friend,
For when you falter, you confess,
You seek forgiveness, change your ways,
And strive to fix the brokenness.

And as I ponder all these things,
I wonder if I, too, could be
The kind of friend that you deserve,
A soul as kind, as pure, as free.

세월은 그렇게 왔다 그렇게 가더이다

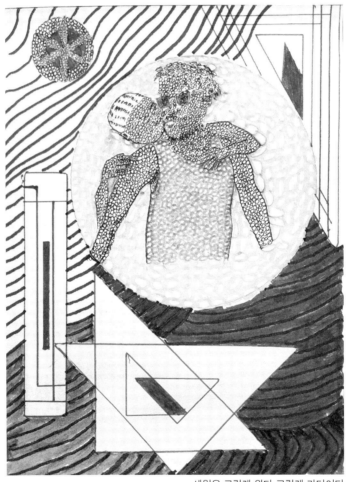

세월은 그렇게 왔다 그렇게 가더이다

이 세상의 모든 여인에게

여자는 꽃처럼 아름답다
여자는 물처럼 부드럽고 바위처럼 단단하다

여자는 강하고 강하다
여자는 연하고 연하다
그리고 참고 또 참는다

여자는 사랑을 주고 또 주고
아낌없이 베풀고 용서하고 또 용서한다

비바람 눈보라 속에서는 따뜻하게 감싸안고
한여름 무더위에는 시원한 바람 되는 여인

여인의 사랑은 늘 푸른 소나무처럼 변함이 없다
여인은 개미처럼 작고 가냘프지만 끊임없이 일을 한다
여인의 존재는 코끼리처럼 크지만 타인에게 위해를 가하지 않는다
여인은 황소처럼 관절이 닳도록 일하지만 불평이 없다
여인은 바보처럼 순한 눈으로 세상을 보지만 현명하고 관대하여라

꽃처럼 아름다운 여인
물처럼 부드러운 여인
바위처럼 단단한 여인이

세상을 구원한다

To All the Women of This World

A woman is as beautiful as a flower,
Soft as water, yet strong as stone.
In her strength, she is unyielding,
In her gentleness, tender beyond compare,
And ever she endures.

She gives love, and gives again,
She forgives and forgives once more,
Pouring forth her kindness,
Without a second thought,
Her heart an endless well of grace.

In storms of rain and biting snow,
She wraps us warm within her arms.
In the heat of summer's fiercest sun,
She is the breeze that cools the air.

Her love is like the evergreen pine,
Unchanging through the seasons,
Though small as an ant and delicate in frame,
She toils on, without complaint,
Her presence vast, like the elephant's,

Though she harms no living soul.

She labors, her hands worn like a farmer's plough,
Yet speaks no word of discontent.
She gazes at the world with gentle eyes,
Seeming simple, yet wise beyond measure.

A woman, fair as a flower in bloom,
Soft as the flowing stream,
And steadfast as the mountain's stone—
It is she who saves the world.

세월은 그렇게 왔다가 그렇게 가더이다

밤의 깊은 어둠 속에 아늑함이 배어 있고
고난과 시련 속에 희망의 불씨가 담겨 있고
사랑의 짧은 불꽃 뒤에 긴 이별의 슬픔이 있다는 것을
세월이 흐른 뒤에야 알겠더이다

찬란했던 젊음도
변치 않을 것 같은 인연도
잠깐의 환희와 슬픔만 남기고 그렇게 가더이다

끈질겼던 가난도
이유 없이 찾아왔던 미움도
세월이 지나니 그렇게 지나가더이다

땀 흘려 정상에 오르지만
세상을 내려다보는 기쁨도 잠시
다시 내려와야만 하더이다

욕심을 버리면 행복해진다 했는데
욕심을 내려놓으니
먹는 즐거움도
멋진 옷 멋진 집 멋진 차
멋진 미래도 함께 내려놓아야겠더이다

우리는 끝없는 연민과 모순 속에서
자기 편한 대로 짜맞추며 살아야겠더이다

그렇게 세월은 바람처럼 왔다가
강물처럼 흘러가더이다

Thus Time Came and Thus It Passed

In the deep silence of the night,
There is a softness that seeps within,
And in trials and hardships,
There lies the spark of hope, unseen.
Only with the passing years,
Do we come to know—
That after love's brief flame,
Comes the long sorrow of farewell.

Youth, once radiant and bright,
And bonds that seemed unbreakable,
Leave behind but fleeting moments
Of joy and grief,
And then they, too, pass.

The stubborn weight of poverty,
The unprovoked sting of hatred,
These, too, with time,
Fade like a distant storm.

We climb the peaks,
Sweat dripping from our brows,
But the joy of standing tall,

Of gazing upon the world below,

Is brief—

For we must descend again.

They say,

"To let go of desire is to find happiness,"

And so I've set my longings free.

Yet in doing so,

I have also let go of the joys—

The taste of a fine meal,

The pleasure of fine clothes,

A beautiful home, a shining car,

And dreams of a grand tomorrow.

In endless contradiction and sympathy,

We weave our lives together,

Each strand pulled to suit our comfort,

And in that way, we continue on.

Thus, time came like the wind,

And flowed like the river,

Passing quietly by,

As all things do.

무명 시절

눈에 안 띄는 곳에서 눈길을 주지 않아도
예쁘게 피었다 시드는 이름 모를 풀꽃

그림자로 살면서
밝은 곳에선 짓밟히고
어둠 속에선 없어지는 존재

이름이 없다는 것은 궁핍입니다
이름을 알리기까지 얼마나 더 기다려야 하나
준비된 자만이 카이로스*를 만날 수 있습니다

고흐는 무명 시절 절망하여 귀를 잘라야 했고
카미유 클로델은 로댕에게 버림받아
천재성을 빛내지 못하고 무명으로 끝내야 했습니다

이름 없음은 더 많은 노력과
땀을 흘려야 한다는 뜻입니다
무명으로 살다 간 수많은 예술가들과
학자들이 남기고 간 작품들이
햇볕을 받아 싹이 트면
사람들은 버릇처럼 물을 주고
거름을 주어 꽃피게 합니다

언젠가는 모래 속에서 보석처럼 반짝이고
쓰레기 더미 속에 핀 빨간 장미처럼 아름다울 것입니다
무명 시절은 도전의 시절이고 잃을 게 없는 시절입니다
옥탑방에서 세상을 보고 있지만
그들의 꿈은 무지개색으로 세상을 바꾸는 것입니다

* 카이로스: 결정적이고 중요한 기회의 순간.

The Time of Obscurity

In places where no eyes wander,
Where no gaze lingers,
A nameless wildflower blooms,
And quietly withers, unseen.

Living in the shadows,
Tread upon in the light,
And vanishing in the darkness,
A fleeting presence,
Unremarked.

To be without a name
Is a kind of poverty—
How long must I wait
Until my name finds its way into the world?
Only those prepared
May seize their moment of kairos.*

Van Gogh, in his nameless years,
Despaired and took the blade to his ear.
Camille Claudel, abandoned by Rodin,
Her genius buried in silence,
Never to be seen.

To live without a name
Is to labor harder,

To sweat unseen,
Like the countless artists and scholars before,
Whose works lie dormant,
Waiting for the sun to break the soil.

And when their names, like seeds,
Begin to sprout beneath that warmth,
People will tend them—
Water them,
Feed them,
Until they bloom,
Almost as if they always had.

Someday, like a jewel gleaming in the sand,
Like a red rose blossoming amidst the refuse,
They too will shine.
The time of obscurity
Is a time of challenge,
A time with nothing left to lose.

Though they gaze upon the world from the rooftop,
Their dreams will color the sky,
And change it with hues of the rainbow.

* Kairos: A moment of critical opportunity or significance.

개 같은 인생

개를 키우는 것은
자식을 키우고
친구를 만들고
사랑을 키우는 것입니다

개는 해바라기처럼 주인만 바라보고 삽니다
언제 보아도 꼬리를 치며 반갑다 인사합니다
개에게 한번 주인은 영원한 주인이 되어
변함없는 충성심을 보입니다

개 같은 소리한다
나쁜 말 아닙니다
개는 본대로 사실만을 말합니다
거짓말을 할 줄 모릅니다

개 같은 놈 나쁜 욕 아닙니다
개는 충성스럽고 배신을 안 합니다
개 같은 놈 나쁜 욕 아닙니다

개무시한다
나쁜 말 아닙니다
낯선 개는 으르렁거리며 물까 봐 겁나서 무시할 수 없고

우리 집 개는 꼬리를 살랑대며 반갑다 하는데
어찌 무시할 수가 있습니까

개 같은 짓 하지 마라
나쁜 짓 아닙니다
개는 주인 명령에 절대복종하고
함께 외출하면 호위무사가 됩니다

개는 인간의 장난감이 아닙니다
소중히 다루어야 할 생명체입니다
개를 사랑하는 사람은 개와 눈으로 대화하고
가슴으로 사랑을 나눕니다

개에게 기쁨이란 당신의 존재입니다
당신과 동행하는 것이 그들의 행복입니다
개에게 욕심이란 오로지 당신에게 사랑을 받는 것입니다
개 같은 인생 나쁘지 않습니다

A Dog's Life

To raise a dog
Is to raise a child,
To find a friend,
To nurture love itself.

A dog, like the sunflower,
Turns always toward its master,
Greeting them with a wagging tail,
In joyful anticipation, without end.
To the dog, a master once given
Is a master forever,
A loyalty unwavering, a bond unbroken.

They say, "You speak like a dog,"
But is that such a curse?
Dogs speak only the truth,
For they do not know how to lie.

"You're like a dog," they say—
Yet, is that so wrong?
For dogs are faithful,
And they never betray.
To be called "dog"
Is to be called true.

To "ignore a dog," they say,

But how could I?
For even the unknown dog growls with fear,
And the dog of my house wags with love—
How could I turn away from such devotion?

They say, "Don't act like a dog,"
But a dog's actions are never wrong.
It obeys its master's every word,
And becomes a warrior by their side,
Guarding with its heart.

A dog is not a toy,
But a living soul to be cherished.
Those who love dogs speak with their eyes,
And share their hearts through quiet gestures.

For a dog's joy is found in you—
Your presence, your companionship.
Its only desire is to receive your love,
To live in your affection.

A dog's life—
It is not so bad.
To live as purely,
As truly,
As a dog.

우릴 가난케 하는 것

낙조로 서산이 황혼으로 불타고 있는데
함께 감탄할 사람 없고
산사로 가는 숲속 길이 눈에 덮여 있어도
동행할 친구 없으니 나는 가난하다

가을이 깊어 앞뜰 감나무에 홍시가 까치밥이 되어가도
내 곁을 떠난 그대 소식이 없으니 가슴이 가난해진다

가난은 몰두하게 한다
일에 몰두하든 절약에 몰두하든
사랑에 몰두하든

빛이 가난해지면 어두움이 찾아오고
자유가 가난해지면 독재를 낳고
정의가 가난해지면 부패를 낳고
사랑이 가난해지면 편견과 증오를 낳는다

아침 밥상에 우유가 떨어졌어요
버스 타고 갈 차비가 없어요
전기세를 못 내서 단전이 됐어요
이런 익숙한 소리들은 가난을 초라하게 한다

요행을 바라면 가난은 더 비참해지고
가난은 부자가 되어야 벗어나는 것이 아니라
가난과 함께할 때 벗어날 수 있다

시간이 가난해지면 일찍 죽고
마음이 가난해지면 모든 것을 잃는다

나이 들어 열정은 식고
반겨줄 사람이 없으니 인생이 가난해진다

나는 가난하다
가난한 친구가 찾아와서
가난한 밥상을 내왔지만 부자처럼 먹었다

가난 그 피할 수 없는 굴레요
우릴 가난케 하여 범사에 감사해하며 살게 하소서

What Makes Us Poor

The sunset burns the western hills in twilight,
But there is no one to share the wonder with,
The forest path to the temple is blanketed in snow,
But without a friend to walk beside me, I am poor.

Autumn deepens, and the persimmons ripen on the boughs,
Left for the birds to eat,
Yet with no word from you,
The absence fills my heart with poverty.

Poverty drives us to focus—
On work, on saving,
Or on love.

When light grows poor, darkness finds its way,
When freedom is scarce, it births tyranny,
When justice withers, corruption takes its place,
And when love runs dry, prejudice and hatred grow.

"We're out of milk for breakfast,"
"There's no fare for the bus today,"
"The power's been cut; we couldn't pay the bill."
Such familiar sounds,

Make poverty feel so bleak, so small.

When we wish for luck,
Poverty deepens its hold.
We do not escape poverty by becoming rich,
But by learning to live alongside it.

When time grows poor, life is cut short.
When the heart grows poor,
Everything is lost.

Growing old, my passion fades,
And with no one to greet me,
Life itself feels impoverished.

I am poor—
But when a poor friend comes to visit,
We share a humble meal,
And eat like kings.

Poverty, that inescapable yoke,
Makes us poor,
Yet teaches us gratitude for all things.

Carpe diem(오늘을 잡아라)

편의점에서 아르바이트하면서 삼각김밥으로 점심
라면 한 봉지로 저녁을 때우고
밤새워 독서실에서 공부하며 미래를 꿈꾸는 젊은이

중풍으로 쓰러진 부인을 주물러주고
운동시켜 주면서 조금씩 나아지는 모습에 감사 기도하는 할아버지

새벽에 우유배달 낮에는 건물 청소하면서
아들딸 대학 공부시키려
뼈 빠지게 일하면서도 웃음을 잃지 않는 홀어머니

세상에 빛과 소금이 되어 하루를 보내는 사람들
지금 비록 힘들지만 최선을 다했을 때
오늘이 내 운명의 하루가 된다

창문 틈으로 들어오는 밝은 햇살
새들의 청량한 울음소리
손녀딸이 켜는 바이올린 소리
흐르는 세월 속에 묻혀
오늘도 흘러가겠지만
나에게 주어진 하루를 오롯이 내 것으로 만들어야지

Carpe Diem

In the corner store, a young soul works,
Lunch is a samgak gimbap,
Dinner a simple bag of noodles,
Dreaming of futures while studying late
In the quiet of the night.

An old man kneads his wife's weary limbs,
Grateful for each small sign of recovery,
As he guides her through gentle exercises,
Whispering prayers of thanks.

A mother rises before dawn,
Delivering milk, cleaning buildings by day,
Laboring tirelessly to send her children
To college, yet she carries a smile,
A beacon of resilience in her toil.

They are the salt and light of the earth,
Living each day with purpose,
Though the struggle is real,
Each moment of effort shapes today
Into a day of destiny.

Bright sunlight filters through the window,
The sweet songs of birds fill the air,
And the tender notes of a granddaughter's violin
Drift through the hours,
Beneath the flow of time.
Today may pass like all others,
But I will seize this gift of hours,
And claim it wholly as my own.

당신을 알고부터

내 가슴에 꿈을 심어 준 당신은 누구십니까
내 삶을 은혜로 가득 차게 한 당신은 누구십니까
내 영혼을 빛나게 한 당신은 누구십니까

당신을 알고부터
미소를 배웠습니다
수줍음을 배웠고
사랑을 배웠고
기다림을 배웠습니다

당신을 알고부터
꽃의 아름다움에 눈떴고
떨어지는 낙엽에 쓸쓸함을 느꼈고
새들의 지저귐에서 달콤한 상상을 하게 되고
당신의 미소가 사랑의 침묵임을 알게 되었습니다

당신을 알고부터
꿈을 꾸기 시작했고
당신과 함께 흰 눈 위에 첫 발자국을 남김에 가슴 설레었고
걷는 길이 외롭지 않았고
일기장이 감성의 충만함으로 가득 찼습니다

당신을 알고부터
밤하늘의 별들은 더 반짝였고
낙엽 쌓인 공원의 빈 벤치는 더 쓸쓸해 보였고
창문을 두드리는 거친 바람에도 가슴이 뛰었고
거울 앞에 서는 시간이 많아졌습니다

외로웠던 지난날의 추억도 아름답게 느껴지고
당신과 함께 한 오늘에 감사하게 되고
미래는 민들레 홀씨처럼 번창할 거라
생각하니 가슴이 뜁니다

Since Knowing You

Who are you, who planted dreams within my heart?
Who filled my life with grace, a sacred art?
Who made my soul to shine with light anew,
As I have come to know and cherish you?

Since knowing you, I learned the warmth of smiles,
The sweet embrace of shyness, love that beguiles.
I learned the tender weight of waiting's call,
And in your presence, I found beauty's thrall.

Awake to flowers' grace, my senses stirred,
In falling leaves, I felt a loneliness unheard.
The chirping birds would weave sweet dreams in flight,
And in your smile, I found love's silent light.

Since knowing you, my dreams took flight and soared,
With you beside me, on the snow we've explored,
Leaving first footprints upon the winter's white,
No longer lonely, my heart took to the light.

The stars above now sparkle with a glow,
And empty benches in the park feel the woe,

Yet even as the rough winds knock on my door,

I find my pulse quickening more and more.

Memories of solitude now shine with grace,

And in this day with you, I find my place.

I think of futures blossoming like dandelion seeds,

And my heart leaps with the joy of hope it feeds.

가을은 어디에 숨어 있는가

산은 불타고 있고
도시는 물에 잠기고
지구는 뜨거워져
사람들은 숨 막혀한다

가을은 어디에 숨어 있는가
높고 푸른 가을 하늘
상쾌하고 맑은 공기
선선한 가을바람
어디로 빼돌렸나
자연의 뜻인가
인간의 자작극인가

지구가 치매에 걸렸나
인간의 인내에 과부하가 걸렸나

매미도 지쳐 있고
호랑나비도 맨드라미도 지쳐 있다
전설이 된 가을은 다시 안 돌아오려나

누구 가을이 있는 곳을 아는 사람이 있나요
그동안 인간이 얼마나 사치하고 오만했는지 반성하고 있으니

가을이여 진노하심을 풀고 돌아와

풍성한 계절을 우리가 다시 누릴 수 있도록 해 주십시오

Where Is Autumn Hidden?

The mountains burn with fire,

Cities drown in floods,

The Earth grows hot,

And people gasp for breath.

Where is autumn hiding?

The lofty, azure sky of fall,

The crisp and clear air,

The gentle autumn breeze—

Where have they been concealed?

Is this the will of nature,

Or a farce of humankind?

Has the Earth succumbed to madness?

Is humanity's patience stretched beyond its bounds?

The cicadas wearied,

The tiger butterflies and marigolds too,

Has the autumn, now a legend,

Decided never to return?

Is there anyone who knows where autumn lies?

As we reflect on how indulgent and proud we have been.

O autumn, release your wrath,

And return to us,

That we may once again

Revel in your bounteous season.

동행

같은 시대에 산다는 것
같은 언어를 사용하고
같은 드라마를 보고
울고 웃고 한다면
우린 동행자입니다

야구장에서 축구장에서
함께 즐거하고 슬퍼하고 분개하는 사람들은 동행자입니다

독재자를 미워하고
약한 자를 돕고
의로운 자를 상 주는 것에 동행합니다

고급 차를 끌고 가는 부자가
앞에서 폐지를 가득 실은 리어카를
힘들게 끌고 가는 노인에게 길을 막고 있다고
빵빵 경적을 울려대면 동행이 아닙니다

때로는 손을 잡아주고
때로는 뒤에서 밀어도 주고
무거운 짐 나누어지면서
같은 방향으로 가는 게 동행입니다

부처님의 자비로운 미소와 동행하면서
프란시스코의 평화의 기도와
동행하면서 살기를 원합니다

내 편이 되어준 사람들
나도 그들 편이 되어 같은 목표를 향해갑니다

Companionship

To dwell in this shared time,
To speak the same language,
To watch the same dramas unfold—
Crying and laughing together,
We are companions on this journey.

In the ballparks and fields,
We share joy and sorrow,
Anger and elation;
Those who rally against the tyrant,
And aid the weak,
Together, we walk in pursuit of righteousness.

Yet when the wealthy glide past,
In their luxurious chariots,
Blocking the path of an old man
Straining beneath a cart of refuse,
Honking loudly in disdain—
This is not companionship.

Sometimes, we grasp each other's hands,
Sometimes we offer a gentle push,

Sharing the weight of burdens,

Moving together toward the same horizon—

That is true companionship.

I wish to walk in the light of the Buddha's smile,

To share in the prayer of Francis,

Living in harmony with peace,

As we journey forth together.

For those who have stood by my side,

I, too, shall stand with them,

Together, we shall pursue a common goal,

In this intricate tapestry of life.

느낍니다

장마 뒤 계곡의 우렁찬 물소리에서
거친 파도가 바위에 부딪치며 일으키는 물보라에서
자연의 경외감을 느낍니다

강보에 싸인 갓난아기의 천진스러운 미소에서
인간은 선할 수밖에 없음을 느낍니다

뒤뚱거리며 엄마 오리를 일렬로 따라가는 새끼 오리의 행렬에서
이른 새벽 암탉의 청량한 울음소리에서
생명의 신비를 느낍니다

아무리 냉정한 사람이라도 간곡한 사랑 앞에서
당신도 어쩔 수 없었으리라 느낍니다

인간은 신과 동행할 때
자유를 느끼고 평안함을 느낍니다
인간과 자연이 동행할 때
푸른 하늘을 볼 수 있고
맑은 공기를 마실 수 있을 때
자연과의 공존이 인류가 살아남을 수 있는
유일한 방법이 아닐까 느껴집니다

I Feel It

From the roaring streams that swell after the rain,
In the crashing waves that kiss the rocky shore,
I feel the awe of nature's grand refrain.

In the gentle smile of a swaddled babe,
I sense the goodness that in us must abide,
A purity that no darkness can deprave.

In the waddling line of ducklings, soft and meek,
And the clear crow of a hen at break of dawn,
I find the mystery of life we seek.

For even the coldest heart, before love's plea,
Must yield, must soften, in the face of grace,
In the presence of love's fervent decree.

When man walks side by side with the divine,
He finds in that communion peace profound,
And in nature's embrace, under the blue sky's line,
Breathes air that is pure, his spirit unbound.
I sense that to coexist is our truest way,
To survive as one with the earth and the sea,
In harmony with nature, we must learn to stay,
For this union is the key to our destiny.

스티브 잡스처럼 생각하기

배고픔이
목마름이
살아 있는 것을 움직이게 합니다

사랑에 굶주림
정에 굶주림
관심의 굶주림이
관계를 맺게 합니다

보고 싶음이
설레는 마음이
간직하고 싶음이
사랑의 시작인 것입니다

해와 달이 바뀌고
바람이 나뭇잎을 흔들고
익은 사과가 떨어지고
새싹이 돋고
꽃이 피는 것에서 창작의 영감을 받습니다

음악에서
그림에서

철학과 역사에서
인간의 한숨 소리에서 영감을 얻어 아이디어가 생깁니다

눈에 보이지 않는 미래를 위해
씨를 뿌리고
키우고
경쟁합니다

작은 것에서 위대함이 나오고
거친 것에서 아름다움이 나옵니다

단순한 감동과 동감
움직임이 세상을 바꿉니다

Thinking Like Steve Jobs

It is hunger

and thirst

that stir the essence of life.

A yearning for love,

an aching for connection,

the longing for attention

forge our bonds.

Desire to see,

the thrill of anticipation,

the wish to hold—

these are the seeds of love.

As the sun and moon exchange their places,

the wind sways the leaves,

ripened apples drop,

and new sprouts emerge,

the bloom of creation inspires.

From music,

from painting,

from philosophy and history,

even from the sighs of humanity,

ideas are born.

For the unseen future,

we sow seeds,

tend them,

and compete in their growth.

Greatness springs from the smallest things,

and beauty arises from the rough and unrefined.

Simple emotions and shared feelings,

these movements shall change the world.

스치고 지나온 것들

어머님의 하염없는 사랑을
아버님의 고뇌에 찬 눈빛을 스치고 지나쳐 왔습니다

아내의 집안사 무거운 짐 모르는 척
환자들의 아픈 사연을 듣고 연민의 소통 없이 스치고 지나왔습니다

이웃들의 따뜻한 미소
아파트 경비 아저씨의 아침 인사
청소 아줌마의 땀방울
함께 일했던 직원들의 즐거운 하루 외침도 스치며 지나왔습니다

세상사 거칠었지만 모른 척
아내의 눈물이 내 눈물이 아니라고 스치며 지나왔습니다

차이콥스키의 교향곡
새들의 지저귐
떠다니는 흰 구름
계절의 꽃들을 스치고 지나왔습니다

팔십에 가까운 이 나이까지 손님인 양
스치고 지나왔습니다

모든 것을 스치고 지나쳐 오니

육신도 비어 있고

영혼도 비어 있습니다

The Things That Passed Me By

I've passed through the endless love of my mother,
And the gaze of my father, heavy with pain.
I've skirted the burdens my wife carries,
And the stories of patients' grief,
Without a thread of compassion shared.

The warm smiles of neighbors,
The morning greetings from the watchman,
The sweat of the cleaning lady,
The joyful cries of colleagues,
All brushed past me, unheeded.

Though life's trials were harsh,
I turned my back on their weight,
Even as my wife's tears fell,
I convinced myself they were not my own.

Through Tchaikovsky's symphonies,
The sweet songs of birds,
The drifting white clouds,
And the flowers of each changing season,
I've merely brushed by.

Reaching this age, near eighty,

Like a guest, I've merely passed through.

Having glided through all things,

Both body and spirit lie empty,

A husk adrift in the currents of time,

Devoid of the essence of what it means to be alive.

그런 친구 못 보셨나요

친구

칠월의 어느 날

게으름을 피우다 느지막하게
밖에 나와 보니
해가 중천에 떠 있습니다

뒤뜰에 풀어 놓은 닭들은 장독대 주위에서
졸린 듯 눈을 감고 있습니다

강아지는 문 옆에서 배를 깔고
살점 하나 없는 뼈다귀를 빨고 있습니다

가끔씩 까치가 울다 가고
들판에선 밭을 갈고 있는 경운기 소리가 들립니다

들판에선 새참 소쿠리를 이고 가는
옆집 아주머니가 멀리 보입니다

한여름 산들바람이
텅 빈 마을을 헤집고 다니고 있습니다

옥수수 잎을 살짝살짝 흔들어 놓고는
맨드라미 백일홍의 빨간 매력을 흔들고 있습니다

장마가 끝난 칠월의
무더운 어느 날
나는 고요한 마을의 주인이 되어
이 평온함을 즐기고 있습니다

One Day in July

After yielding to the slow pull of idleness,

I step outside, where the sun hangs heavy in the zenith—

A steady presence, indifferent to time.

The chickens in the yard, loosed from their quiet coop,

Circle the ancient earthen jars,

Their eyes half-shut, drifting between wakefulness and dream.

By the door, the dog lays flat upon the ground,

Gnawing a bare bone, savoring what little remains—

As though time itself were drawn out, stretched thin.

A magpie's cry pierces the air,

An echo of a world beyond this stillness,

While the steady hum of the tiller in the fields

Becomes the heartbeat of the distant land.

Far off, a neighbor woman walks the horizon,

A basket balanced on her head—

Carrying the humble offering of life's small, persistent duties.

The summer breeze, as if unsure of its own purpose,

Moves through the empty village,

Its touch like a question upon the corn leaves,

A soft disturbance upon the red blooms of cockscomb and
zinnia—

A brief reminder of time's quiet insistence.

And here, in this July, after the long rains,

I, the temporary steward of this tranquil world,

Hold within me the fullness of this stillness,

And in its silence, I am cradled.

방귀 소리

방귀를 뀌었느냐
예 그렇습니다
시원하냐
예 시원합니다
네가 시원하면
듣는 사람은 그만큼 고통스럽느니라

장군죽비 맛이 어떠냐
소리는 요란한데 아프지는 않습니다

원래 죄란 죄를 짓는 과정이 요란하지
죄 자체는 미미할 때가 많으니라

스님
이곳에는 목탁 소리
풍경 소리 바람 소리
새소리 시냇물 소리밖에 없는데
무슨 죄를 짓겠습니까

그렇지 않다
하는 일 없이 숨 쉬는 것도 죄요
나눔 없이 혼자만 먹는 것도 죄요

땀 흘린 노동 없이 등 펴고 자는 것도 죄이니라

The Sound of a Fart

"Did you let out that sound?"

"Yes, I did."

"Did it bring you relief?"

"Yes, a great relief."

"But remember, if you find comfort,

Those who hear must bear the weight of that burden."

"And how does the monk's disciplinary staff feel?"

"The sound is loud, but the pain does not linger."

"Such is the nature of sin—

The process of committing it echoes loudly,

Yet the sin itself is often small, almost insignificant."

"Master,

Here, there is only the sound of the wooden bell,

The wind through the pines,

The rustle of the leaves,

Birds calling to one another, and the stream flowing softly.

What sin could be found in such a place?"

"You are mistaken.

Even the act of breathing without purpose can be sin,

To eat alone without sharing is sin,

To rest your back without labor,

Without the sweat of honest toil—

That too, is a sin."

지퍼

지퍼는 옷 입는데 마지막 순서다
신체의 쑥스러운 부분을 가려주지만
엇물리면 여간 성가신 게 아니다

명품 가방이나 옷의 지퍼는 모양도 예쁘고 견고하다
지퍼가 고장 나면 더 이상 명품이 아니다

나이가 들면 눈과 귀 그리고 손이 지퍼로 채워져야 한다
보아도 못 본 척
들어도 못 들은 척
예쁘다고 함부로 손을 대서는 안 된다

지퍼가 헐거우면 삶이 고단해진다
지퍼가 잘 잠겨져 있어야 속이 따뜻하다

지하철 노인석에 앉아 있는데
앞에 서 있던 청년이 귓속말로
할아버지 지퍼가 열려 있어요
얼른 지퍼를 올렸다
정신 나간 늙은이란 소리 안 들으려면
지퍼 단속을 잘하여야 한다

The Zipper

The zipper, the final act of dressing,
Shields the body's modest parts from view,
Yet if it falters, how troublesome the affair!

On bags of finest make or garments rare,
The zipper gleams with grace and strength combined,
But should it break, no longer prized it stands—
For what is luxury, if not intact?

With age, our eyes, our ears, our hearts must too
Be sealed with zippers firm and true.
See not, though you gaze; hear not, though you listen,
And never touch what tempts you with beauty bright,
For all things grow fragile, and careful hands
Must now secure the seams of life.

A loosened zipper makes for weariness,
Life's fabric frays, and cold winds creep within.
But fastened tight, the warmth endures,
And comfort follows where we tread.

On the subway, in the elder's seat I rest,
A young man leans and whispers in my ear,
"Sir, your zipper is undone."
Quickly I pull it closed—
For in this life, if I would stay composed,
I must attend the zippers of my days,
Lest the world declare me lost in time.

구속된다

여섯 살 손녀딸의 천진난만한 미소가
날 구속한다

알뜰살뜰 생활하는 내 처가
생활비가 떨어졌다고 하소연할 때
나는 구속된다

직장 상사가 이달 말까지 진행 중인 프로젝트를
완료하라 지시할 때 나는 구속된다

인간은 정에 구속되고
약속에 구속되고
돈에 구속되고
시간에 구속되고
자연에 구속된다

신의 은총에 구속될 때
부모의 관심과 보호에 구속될 때
당신의 사랑이 날 구속할 때
난 행복해지고 완전해진다

Bound

My six-year-old granddaughter's innocent smile
Binds me, holds me fast in its tender light.

When my wife, so careful and kind,
Whispers of the household bills running dry,
I find myself bound, tied by her need.

When my boss commands the project complete
By the end of the month, I am bound—
By duty, by work, by expectation.

Man is bound by affection,
By promises made,
By the pull of money,
By the ticking of time,
And by the forces of nature itself.

But when I am bound by the grace of God,
Held by the care and protection of my parents,
Bound by the love you offer me—
Then I am happy,
Then I am whole.

세월이 흘러가네

세월은 막무가내로
값을 지불하라고 하네

바람처럼 스쳐 갔건
바위처럼 굴러갔건
시냇물처럼 흘러갔건
머물다 간 세월에 대해 값을 지불하라 하네

머물다 간 세월 동안
따스한 햇볕 받으며 사과는 익어 갔고
우연히 만난 인연으로 사랑도 했다

세월은 시련을 몰고 오기도 하고
이별을 강요하기도 하고
상처를 주기도 하여

사람들은 한 번쯤은 방황도 했고
한 번쯤은 무언가를 버려야 했고
잊어야 했고
외로워져야 했다

그가 왜 사랑한다 말해 놓고

쓸쓸히 떠나야 했는지 이해해야 한다

Time Flows On

Time, relentless, demands its due,

A payment for the days gone by.

Whether it rushed like the wind,

Or rolled like a boulder down a hill,

Or flowed as gently as a stream—

Still, it calls for its price,

For every moment that has passed.

In the warmth of those fleeting days,

Apples ripened beneath the sun,

And love bloomed by chance encounters,

Softly weaving its way through our lives.

Time brought trials, and with them,

Partings we did not choose.

It left scars, deep and unseen,

And led us to wander,

To cast off burdens,

To forget what once was,

And to sit in the quiet of solitude.

Yet we must understand,

Why he said "I love you"

Before leaving in silence,

Loneliness his only companion.

칠월의 정경

장마 뒤 개울물 넘쳐흐르고
먼 산에 뻐꾸기 소리 메아리처럼 들린다
들판엔 잠자리 떼 지어 날고
매미 소리 요란하다

빨간 넝쿨장미 눈부시게 피어 있고
담장 안 게으른 강아지 오수를 즐기고 있다

시집간 딸 불쑥 찾아와 시원한 냉면 만들어 먹자 하고
아들 내외 찾아와 여름휴가로 여행을 떠난다며
부족한 여행 경비를 보태달라고 하여 더운 날씨를 더욱 뜨겁게 한다

손자 성화에 시냇가에 나와 잡히지 않는
송사리 피라미를 잡고 있다
육모정 정자에 동네 노인들 모여
수박 냉채 잡수시며 연신 부채질을 하고 계신다

공포영화에 아이스크림도
흐르는 땀을 막을 수가 없다

그래도 빨리 크고 무성해지는 칠월이 좋다
더위 탓하며 오수를 즐길 수 있어 좋고

시원한 바람을 기다릴 수 있어 좋고
낮잠을 자고 나도 여전히 대낮이어서 좋다

A Scene in July

After the rains, the stream overflows,

And the cuckoo's call from distant hills

Echoes through the valley, clear and soft.

In the fields, dragonflies dance in swarms,

While cicadas hum, their chorus loud and ceaseless.

Bright red roses climb the walls,

Their blooms dazzling under the sun,

And within the yard, a lazy dog

Enjoys his midday slumber in the heat.

My daughter, married and grown,

Arrives unexpectedly with a smile,

Suggesting we make cold noodles, refreshing and light.

My son and his wife, eager for their summer trip,

Ask for a bit more to fund their journey,

Turning the hot day into one of greater heat.

By the stream, at my grandson's request,

I reach for minnows and fish,

Though none will yield to my hand.

At the old pavilion, elders gather—

Watermelon in hand, they fan themselves,

Savoring the coolness of their simple feast.

Even the ice cream melts,

No match for the warmth that clings to the day,

And no ghostly tale can cool the sweat that flows.

Yet, still, I love this swift-growing, verdant July,

For I can blame the heat and enjoy my midday rest.

I love to wait for the cool breeze to come,

And even after a nap,

The day remains—bright and full,

A gift that lingers long into the afternoon.

내 것

나를 보배로 생각하는 우리 어머니
어깨 처진 나를 사랑하는 나의 처
이 세상의 모든 아름답고
귀한 것들은 내 것이다

도서관 있는 책들 속에 들어 있는 스토리와 지식
박물관에 전시되어 있는 예술품들
거리에서 카페에서 들려오는 감미로운 음악은 다 내 것이다

엉뚱한 것에 대한 집념
시기와 질투
나를 가난케 하는 욕심은 내 것이 아니어야 한다

마음속에 일어나는
행복과 불행
사랑과 미움
기쁨과 슬픔은
오로지 내 것이다

마음속에서 내 것이기를 바라는 모든 것은 내 것이고
마음속에서 내 것이 아니기를 바라는 모든 것은 내 것이 아니다
하지만 영원한 내 것도 내 것이 아닌 것도 없다

하늘에 떠도는 저 구름

아파트 담장에 예쁘게 핀 넝쿨장미

아침잠을 깨우는 처마 밑 참새들의 울음소리는 다 내 것이다

Mine

My mother, who treasures me as a gem,
And my wife, who loves me despite my weary shoulders—
All the beautiful and precious things in this world,
They are mine.

The stories and knowledge contained in books of the library,
The masterpieces displayed in the museum's quiet halls,
The sweet melodies drifting through streets and cafés—
They, too, are mine.

But the stubborn obsession with the absurd,
Envy and jealousy,
And the greed that makes me poor—
These must never be mine.

The joys and sorrows that rise within my heart,
The love and the hatred,
The happiness and the grief—
These are wholly mine,
And mine alone.

What I desire to be mine within the confines of my soul,

Is mine.

And what I wish to cast aside,

Will never belong to me.

Yet nothing is truly mine,

And nothing is ever not mine.

The clouds wandering across the sky,

The vine of roses blooming along the apartment wall,

The sparrows whose morning song stirs me from sleep—

They are all mine.

노인의 외로움

푸른 하늘에 바람 따라 흐르다 없어지는
한 조각 흰 구름 같은 것이 노인의 외로움인가

재래시장 모서리에 오지 않는 손님을 기다리는
국밥집 주인 같은 심정이 외로움인가

온몸을 내보이며 숨을 곳 없이
뻥끗 뻥끗 입만 벌리는 어항 속 금붕어 같은 처지가 노인의 외로움
인가

늙어서
동행자 없이 혼자여서
가진 것이 없어서
외로운 건가

외로움은 고독함이다
자아의 상실감으로
삶의 의지를 상실해 가는 과정이다

노인이여 고독함을 즐겨라
인연으로부터의 자유
과거와 미래로부터의 자유를 즐겨라

어둠 속으로 낙조하기 전
마지막 빛을 발하는 태양처럼 자유로운 영혼에 불을 붙여라

고독을 즐기면 외로움이 벗이 되고
혼자 있음에 자유를 느끼면 자유인이 된다

The Solitude of the Elder

Is the solitude of the elder like a lone white cloud,

Drifting across the blue sky, only to vanish with the wind?

Or is it the heart of a soup vendor

At the corner of the old market, waiting endlessly

For customers who never come?

Is it the plight of the goldfish,

Exposed in its glass tank,

Mouths opening and closing, nowhere to hide,

Nowhere to turn?

Is it because one has grown old,

Left without companions,

Or because one has nothing left—

That they feel this solitude?

Solitude is a quiet isolation,

A gradual loss of self,

A slow fading of life's will,

As it drifts away.

But, old one, embrace this solitude,

Rejoice in the freedom it brings—

Freedom from attachments,

Freedom from both past and future.

Before the light fades completely into the dark,

Ignite your spirit,

Like the setting sun, casting its final, glorious rays.

When you embrace your solitude, it becomes your friend,

And when you find freedom in your aloneness,

You become truly free.

그런 친구 못 보셨나요

평범한 모습
낯익은 얼굴
노타이에 수수한 옷차림
그런 친구 못 보셨나요

수줍어 늘 뒤에 서 있던 친구
미소 지으며 말할 땐 트집 잡아 늘 날 칭찬해 주던 친구

오천 원짜리 막걸리
오천 원짜리 점심값을 본인이 내겠다고 우기는
그런 친구 못 보셨나요

어머님 아버님 돌아가셨을 때는
하룻밤 자면서 위로해 주던 친구

작은 행동으로 나를 감동시켰고
작은 몸짓으로 나를 위로했던
그런 친구 못 보셨나요

자기를 낮추기에 바빠 어쩔 줄 모르던 친구
행여 신세 질까 봐 솔선수범하던
그런 친구 못 보셨나요

소심해서 걷는 뒷모습이 애처롭게 보이지만
따뜻한 심장을 가진
그런 친구 못 보셨나요

세상에 많은 빚을 진 것처럼 무언가 열심히 갚으려 하고
겸손하여 어깨가 처진 그런 친구 못 보셨나요
그가 오래오래 건강하게 살았으면 좋겠습니다

Have You Seen Such a Friend?

A friend, ordinary in appearance,

Familiar in face,

Dressed simply, without a tie—

Have you seen such a friend?

The one who stood shyly in the back,

Smiling as he spoke,

Always finding something kind to say,

Always defending me with gentle words.

The friend who insisted on paying

For the humble lunch,

For the five thousand-won bottle of makgeolli—

Have you seen such a friend?

When my mother and father passed away,

He stayed with me through the night,

Offering comfort in silence,

With small gestures,

Little acts that moved me deeply.

Always lowering himself, unsure where to stand,

Anxious to never impose,

He stepped forward quietly,

Leading by example, without a word.

Though his steps might seem timid,

And his figure fragile,

He carried within him a heart so warm—

Have you seen such a friend?

As if he owed a debt to the world,

He worked tirelessly to repay it,

Shoulders hunched in humility,

Have you seen such a friend?

May he live long, this friend of mine,

With a heart full of grace,

And health to carry his quiet soul.

잔소리

잔소리는 옳은 말 같은데
반복해서 하니 지겹다
편견과 독선이 들어 있는 잔소리는 귀에 거슬린다

세월의 흐름에 따라
잔소리의 양과 질도 달라진다

손녀딸이 잔소리를 한다
할아버지 넘어지지 마세요
건강하게 오래 사세요

어두운 밤 별들의 잔소리
숲속에서 들리는 나뭇잎들의 잔소리
선창가 갈매기들의 잔소리
우리 집 강아지 짖어대는 잔소리
임윤찬이 연주하는 라흐마니노프의 피아노 협주곡

내 심장을 뛰게 하는 사랑의 속삭임
그런 잔소리 끊임없이 듣고 싶다

메아리 없는 잔소리는 서글프고
낯익은 잔소리 없어진 세상은 낯설고 외로워라

Chatter

Chatter, though filled with truth,
Becomes tiresome in its constant refrain.
When tainted by bias and pride,
It grates upon the ear.

With time's steady flow,
The measure and meaning of chatter
Changes, as seasons do.

My granddaughter's tender words,
"Grandfather, don't fall,
Stay healthy and live long"—
Is that not chatter too?

In the quiet of night,
I hear the stars whisper in the sky,
The leaves rustle in the woods,
Seagulls cry by the pier,
And my dog barks at the door—
Chatter, all of it.

Even Rachmaninoff's concerto,
Played by Yunchan Lim,
Becomes a kind of chatter,
Stirring my heart to beat faster.

But oh, the whispers of love,
The endless chatter of affection—
Such noise I wish never to cease.

Chatter without echo is a sorrowful thing,
And a world grown silent of familiar voices—
How strange, how lonely it would be.

달라져야 한다

아무리 울어도 좋은 소식을 가져오지 못하는
앞뜰 미루나무에 터 잡고 살고 있는 까치는 달라져야 한다

아침 새벽에는 안 울고 시도 때도 없이 울어대는
닭장 안의 닭들은 달라져야 한다

당뇨병이 있는데도 단것만 좋아하고
뚱뚱해져가는 나의 처는 달라져야 한다

불의를 보고
모르는 척하고 오히려 부추기는
나와 나의 이웃은 달라져야 한다

습관화된 사랑이 따분해지고
무관심이 당연하게 느껴질 때
무언가 달라져야 한다

주름진 얼굴
퇴행성 관절염으로 절룩거리는 나는
세월의 흐름에 따라 달라져야 한다

There Must Be Change

The magpie that dwells in the tall poplar,
Bringing no good news, though it calls—
It must change.

The chickens, crowing at all hours,
Unbidden at dawn and dusk—
They, too, must change.

My wife, though she loves the sweet things still,
Her body growing heavier each day,
Despite the illness that lingers—
She must change.

I, and my neighbors,
Turning our faces from injustice,
Silent, or worse, feeding the flames—
We must change.

When love becomes a habit,
And indifference feels like the norm,
When all grows stale—
Something must change.

And I, with my wrinkled face,
And my steps now slowed by age,
By time's relentless tide—
I, too, must change.

친구의 방문

그도 늙었지만
나는 더 늙어 있었다
청춘이었을 때는 같은 야망을 가졌었고
중년이었을 때는 같은 시련을 겪었고
노인이 되었을 때는 부족했던 지난날을 함께 후회했던 친구

외로웠던 지난날을 풍요롭게 해주었던 친구가
부족했던 젊은 시절을 채워주었던
나의 친구가 멀리서 방문했다

살아 있음에 축하하고
이루어 놓은 것 없으나
서로의 작은 성취에 칭찬할 수 있는
친구의 방문은 즐거운 일이다

짧은 만남 후 헤어진다 해도
발아하기 전 꽃봉오리로
다시 만날 순 없지만

아프지 말자
마음껏 사랑하며 사랑받으며 살자

A Friend's Visit

He, too, has aged,
But I have grown even older.
In our youth, we shared the same ambitions,
In middle age, we endured the same trials,
And now, as old men, we share the same regrets
For the things we left undone.

A friend who once filled my lonely days
And enriched the empty years of my youth
Has come from afar to visit me.

We celebrate the fact that we are still alive,
Though we have achieved little.
In each other's small victories,
We find joy,
And his visit brings a quiet gladness.

Though our meeting is brief
And we part again,
Like blossoms that will never bloom again,
Still, we understand:
We may not meet in this life once more.

Let us not suffer.
Let us live,
Loving freely and being loved in return.

가야 할 길

가야 할 곳은 정해져 있다
가는 길엔 꽃도 피고
새소리도 들렸는데
앞만 보고 걸었다

헛걸음질도 해보고
헛날갯짓도 해보고
목표가 저긴데 엉뚱한 방향으로 가기도 했다

흐린 날도
맑은 날도
바람처럼 지나쳤다

변방의 겨울바람은 차가웠고
우린 아무 잘못도 없는데
헤어져야 했다
바람에 묻혀 지나가 버린 세월

해는 뉘엿뉘엿 석양에 와 있는데
가야 할 길은 멈추려 해도 멈춰지지 않는
가파른 내리막길

누구 내 갈 길을 막고
더 머물다 가라 붙잡는 사람 없나

The Road Ahead

The road I'm meant to walk is set,
Though flowers bloomed along the path,
And birds called from the trees—
I kept my eyes ahead, and marched.

I stumbled here and there,
Flapping wings in vain,
And strayed where I should not have gone,
With my goal just out of sight.

The days were cloudy, the days were clear,
And both slipped by like wind.
The winter winds from far-off lands
Were bitter cold,
And though we did no wrong,
We had to part—
Time passed on, hidden in the breeze.

The sun now sinks into the west,
And the road that lies ahead
Is steep, and pulling me forward still—
It will not stop, though I might wish to rest.

Is there no one who'll stand before me,

Who'll hold me back,

And ask me to stay a little while longer?

가난한 시인이 된 의사

가난한 시인이 된 의사

가난한 시인이 된 의사

가난하니까 우선 마음이 편하다
뺏길 것도 없고
허세 부릴 것도
숨길 것도 없으니
그렇게 편할 수가 없다

돈 꾸러 오는 사람도 없고
간소한 밥상으로 대접해도 구두쇠라 욕하지 않으니 좋다

육신은 병들고 노쇠하여 환자를 돌볼 수 없는 의사지만
시를 쓴다는 것은
머리와 가슴에 쌓인 연륜과 경험
청년 같은 왕성한 의욕으로 무언가
새로운 것을 만들어 내고 있다는 기쁨이 있다

산에 오르다
꽃이 예쁘다고 꺾지는 않았는지
시냇가 산책로를 걷다가 무심코
개미의 행렬을 밟고 지나가지는 않았는지

비록 지금 가진 것 없지만
이 넘쳐나는 사랑을 나누어 줄

사람은 없는지 살피면서 시를 쓴다

가난은 지혜를 만든다
가난은 꿈을 꾸게 한다
시인은 그것을 노래한다

The Poor Poet Who Was Once a Doctor

In poverty, there is a strange peace.

Nothing to lose,

Nothing to hide,

No mask to wear—

And in this simplicity,

I find a freedom that breathes.

No one knocks at my door for borrowed coins,

And when I offer a humble meal,

No whispers accuse me of greed.

It feels like relief.

Once, my hands tended to the sick,

But now, this aging body

Can no longer heal.

Yet in the act of writing—

I discover a quiet joy.

Here, within my thoughts and heart,

Gathered over the years,

Is the wisdom of life lived.

With the zeal of youth still flickering,

I create something new,

Something that rises from within.

As I walk the mountain's path,
Did I unknowingly pluck a flower,
Admiring its beauty without a second thought?
Or while strolling by the stream,
Did I tread too heavily,
Crushing the delicate trail of ants?

Though I have little,
I look around,
Wondering if there is anyone
To receive the love that overflows from me.

Poverty brings wisdom,
Poverty births dreams,
And the poet sings of this—
Of love, of loss,
Of what it means to be truly alive.

봄소식

봄은 점령군처럼 깃발을 펄럭이며
나팔 소리 요란하게 오지 않는다
수줍은 새색시처럼 살며시 온다

그의 의상은 화려하지만
몸은 추위로 떨고 있고
마음은 아직 새싹이다

봄바람이 꽃 소식보다 먼저 와
잠깐 머물면서
시냇가 버드나무에선 갯버들 솟아나고
앞산 아지랑이 아롱아롱하다

벌판엔 노란 유채꽃이 한창인데
뜸부기 울면 봄이 오려나
나에겐 아직 봄소식이 없다

봄이여 꽃을 든 여인처럼
어서 다가와 가슴에 안기어다오

The Tidings of Spring

Spring does not come
With banners waving,
Nor with trumpets blaring—
It arrives gently,
Like a shy maiden, stepping softly.

Her garments are bright,
Yet her body trembles still with cold,
And her heart remains but a tender bud.

Before the blossoms, the breeze of spring
Arrives, lingering for a moment,
Stirring the willows by the stream,
While mist rises softly from the distant hills.

Across the fields, the yellow canola blooms,
And when the quail calls,
Perhaps spring will truly arrive.
But for me,
There is still no sign of spring.

Oh, Spring!
Like a woman bearing flowers,
Come swiftly,
And fold yourself into my waiting arms.

운명

우리가 이기려 했던 것은 무엇인가요
우리가 참아야 했던 것은 무엇인가요
우리가 속수무책으로 당해야 했던 것은 무엇인가요

자연의 힘을
신의 뜻을 우린 통제할 수 없습니다

우린 단지 배고픔을
성급함을
유혹을
질투나 미움을
조금은 통제할 수 있을 뿐입니다

새벽 첫닭의 울음소리를
서쪽 하늘을 붉게 물들이고
넘어가는 석양을 막을 수 없습니다

얼굴에 주름이 지고
흰머리가 나는
세월의 흐름을 어찌 통제할 수 있겠습니까

만남이 있었고

헤어짐이 있었고
지나간 것은 잊어야 했고
가질 수 없음에 가슴앓이했습니다

사랑했는데 그대는 떠났고
그 빈자리에 그리움만 차 있습니다

Fate

What was it we sought to conquer?

What were we meant to endure?

What was it that, powerless,

We had to suffer through?

The forces of nature,

The will of the divine—

These are beyond our grasp.

We can only control hunger,

Impatience,

Temptation,

A hint of jealousy or hatred—

But only just.

The crow of the first rooster at dawn,

The sun setting in crimson hues beyond the western sky—

These we cannot halt.

The wrinkles on our faces,

The whitening of our hair—

How can we ever hope to stop the passage of time?

There were meetings,

And there were partings.

We had to forget what had passed,

And suffer the ache of what we could not hold.

I loved you,

But you left,

And in your absence, only longing remains.

돈보다 귀한 것

돈보다 귀한 것은
현명한 생각
절제된 행동
공감하고 배려하는 마음이다

돈보다 귀한 것은
엄마의 따뜻한 손길
내 처의 부드러운 미소
자식들의 활기찬 아침 인사다

돈보다 귀한 것은
시간을 아껴 쓰고
취미 삼아 산에 오르고
사랑받고 사랑을 주는 것이다

돈보다 귀한 것은
가치를 지키겠다는 의지
버릴 것은 버리겠다는 용기
고난을 이겨내겠다는 인내심이다

돈보다 귀한 것은
자유로운 생각

더불어 사는 세상
내가 하고 싶은 일을 하는 것이다

돈보다 귀한 것은
앞뜰에 심어놓은 상추
고추 시금치
닭장 안의 닭과
우리 집의 파수꾼
강아지이고
가난한 우리이다

What Is Worth More Than Money

What is worth more than money

Is a wise mind,

Actions held in restraint,

A heart that knows how to care and share.

What is worth more than money

Is a mother's warm touch,

The soft smile of a wife,

The cheerful morning greetings of children.

What is worth more than money

Is time well spent,

Climbing mountains for the joy of it,

Loving and being loved in return.

What is worth more than money

Is the will to guard your values,

The courage to let go when needed,

And the patience to endure hardship.

What is worth more than money

Is the freedom of thought,

A world where we live together,

And the joy of doing what I love.

What is worth more than money

Are the lettuce leaves growing in the garden,

The peppers and spinach,

The chickens in the coop,

And our faithful dog,

Who guards this simple, humble life—

This life, rich in its own way.

힘들 때 기댈 수 있는 사람

키는 150센티미터
몸무게는 40킬로그램
새벽 4시에 일어나 밤 11시가 되어야 잠자리에 드는 여인
비 오는 날 집안에 하나밖에 없는 우산을 들고 배웅 와서
나에게는 우산을 씌워주고 본인은 비를 맞고 가는 여인
나보다 서른세 살이 더 많은 여인
내 나이 오십이 될 때까지 기대어 살았던 여인

나는 그녀의 따뜻한 가슴에 기대었고
그녀의 맑은 영혼에 기대었고
그녀의 지고지순한 희생정신에 기대었고
그녀의 현명함에 기대어 일생을 살았습니다

슬플 때도
억울할 때도
절망할 때도
그녀에게 기대어 위로를 받았고 힘을 얻었습니다

그녀는 떠났습니다
난 기댈 곳을 잃었습니다
추억 속에 남아 있는
그녀의 따뜻한 가슴과

부드러운 손길을 그리워하면서
아직도 기대어 살아갑니다

Someone to Lean on in Difficult Times

She stood barely five feet tall,

Weighed no more than forty kilograms,

Waking at four in the morning,

And only retiring to bed after eleven at night.

On rainy days, she would greet me with the only umbrella we

had,

Holding it above my head

While letting herself be drenched by the rain.

She was thirty-three years my senior,

And I leaned on her until I turned fifty.

I leaned on her warm heart,

On her clear and pure soul,

On her unwavering spirit of sacrifice,

On her wisdom, which guided me throughout my life.

In sorrow,

In frustration,

In despair,

I leaned on her,

Finding comfort and strength in her presence.

But she has left.

And now, I am without a place to lean.

I still long for her warm embrace,

For her gentle touch,

And though she lives now only in my memories,

I continue to lean on those,

Still trying to find my way.

고향 집의 겨울 정경

흰 눈이 소리 없이 내려 장독 위에 하얗게 쌓여 있고
처마 밑 고드름은 점점 커져 땅에 닿을 듯하다

툇마루에는 시래기 줄 졸린 듯 매달려 있고
감나무 위에는 따다 남긴 홍시 몇 개가 자기 크기만 한 눈을 이고 있다

앞뜰의 눈 위에 먹이를 찾는 참새들의 종종걸음 찍혀 있고
미루나무 위의 까치집은 눈에 덮여 있다

이웃집 강아지가 가끔씩 멍멍 짖어대며 정적을 깬다

거실에서는 보는 사람 없이 티브이 켜져 있고
안방 아랫목에서는 노부부가 천 원짜리 화투를 치고 있다

느리고 한가하게 시간은 가고
밤이 오고
닭 우는 소리가 새벽을 깨운다

Winter at the Old Home

White snow falls silently, piling high
Upon the jar-tops in the yard,
While icicles beneath the eaves
Grow longer, reaching down to touch the ground.

On the porch, dried greens hang still,
Drowsy in their winter sleep.
And on the persimmon tree,
A few bright fruits, forgotten and left behind,
Carry on their backs the weight of snow,
As large as they themselves.

In the snow-covered yard,
Sparrows scurry, leaving tiny tracks
As they search for scattered seed.
Above, the magpie's nest lies hidden,
Tucked beneath a blanket of snow.

Now and then, the neighbor's dog barks,
Breaking the heavy silence.

Inside, the TV flickers on,
Though no one watches.
And in the warmest room,
An old couple plays a quiet game of cards,

Each move slow, each gesture soft.
Time drifts by, slow and unhurried,
Until night falls,
And the crowing of a rooster
Calls forth the dawn.

백지의 점 하나

어떤 시인이 백지에 점 하나 찍어 놓고
신 시라고 발표했다

독자와 비평가들은 이게 무엇이지 황당해하다가
흥분해서 떠들어 대기 시작했다
이 얼마나 간결하고 명료한 시적 표현인가

그는 시의 종결자이다
백지의 점 하나에 그의 사상과 행적
인품과 천재성이 다 들어 있다고 추켜세웠다

어떤 비평가는 그가
쉼표도 아니고
느낌표도 아니고
물음표도 아니고 마침표를 찍었다는 것에 의미를 부여했고

영어로도
중국어로도
일본어로도
번역이 필요치 않는
백지의 점 하나로 세계인을 공감시켰고
세계를 평정했다고 시 후감을 썼을지 모르겠다

물음표 하나로 인생을 고민했던 철학자
느낌표 하나로 인생을 노래했던 시인
쉼표 하나 찍어 놓고 일만 하다 죽어간 노동자
우린 모두 마침표 하나 찍어 놓고 인생을 살다 떠나는지 모르겠다

백지에 점 하나 찍어 놓고
푸시킨은 삶이라 하고
워즈워스는 무지개라 하고
롱펠로는 시위를 떠난 화살이라 하고
이백은 술 한 잔이라 하고
정지용은 고향이라 부를 수 있겠다

어떤 비평가는 백지 위의 점 하나를 비평하며
책 한 권을 썼을 게고
사려 깊은 독자들은 백지 위의 점 하나를 음미하며
감격할지도 모르겠다

A Dot on a Blank Page

One day, a poet placed a single dot
On a blank page,
And called it a poem.

Readers and critics, bewildered,
Stared in silence,
Until slowly,
They began to murmur,
To debate,
And finally, to praise:
What simplicity, what purity in expression!

He was the one who ended poetry,
The final voice.
In that one small dot,
They saw the weight of his thought,
The trace of his life,
The essence of his genius.

One critic, perhaps, pondered deeply:
This is not a comma, nor an exclamation,
Not a question or a pause—
But a period.
And in that decision, they found meaning.

No need for translation—
In every language,
That dot spoke its truth.

It captured the world,
The whole world,
In a single stroke.

The philosopher,
Who had wrestled his whole life with questions,
The poet,
Who had sung the sharpness of exclamation,
The laborer,
Who had lived his days in the long pause of commas—
All would end
With a single period.

That single dot—
Pushkin would have called it life,
Wordsworth might have seen a rainbow,
Longfellow, an arrow in flight,
Li Bai, a cup of wine,
And Jeong Ji-yong,
Might have called it home.

Some critics would write endlessly
About that one small dot,
While thoughtful readers
Might sit in quiet awe,
Feeling the depth
Of what was left unspoken.

어둠도 빛이 되더라

빛을 찾다가 빛을 잃었다
하늘의 별들은 검은 구름 뒤에 숨어 있었고
어둠만이 우릴 지배했었다

이정표도 보이지 않았고
GPS도 무용지물이었다
머물 수도 돌아갈 수도 없게 만드는 어둠은 독재자였다

어둠이 주는 고요함
밤이 주는 아늑함은 간데없고
비바람과 천둥번개만이 어둠을 더 길게 깊게 하고 있었다

눈 오는 겨울밤의 하얀 빛
어느 시골 농부의 집 창문을 통해 새어 나오는 은은한 불빛
골목길에서 도시의 비밀을 엿듣고 있는 희미한 가로등이
어둠을 걷어내고 우릴 구원할 수 있을 것 같다

새벽을 깨우는 아침 햇빛
그대를 만난 후 마음속에서 우러나오는 사랑의 불빛
절망을 깨부수는 희망의 불빛

겹겹이 덮인 어둠을 한 겹 한 겹 벗겨내고

이런 빛들로 채워가니
어둠도 빛이 되더라

Even Darkness Becomes Light

In seeking light, I lost it.
The stars in the sky hid behind dark clouds,
And only the darkness reigned over us.

There were no signposts to guide us,
Even GPS was useless.
The darkness became a tyrant,
Leaving us neither a place to stay
Nor a way to turn back.

The calm that night should bring,
The quiet comfort of darkness,
Was nowhere to be found.
Only the storm and thunder,
Stretching the darkness deeper, longer.

But the white glow of snow on a winter's night,
The soft light from the window
Of a distant farmhouse,
The dim streetlight,
Listening to the city's secrets—
These could lift the darkness,

These could save us.

The morning sun that wakes the dawn,
The light of love that fills my heart since I met you,
The glow of hope that shatters despair.

Layer by layer,
The darkness peels away,
Replaced by these lights.
And even darkness,
Becomes light.

인내심

비틀거리는 젊음
무너져 내린 노년
살아가는 것 자체가 인내심이다
인내심은 선택이 아니라 살아야겠다는 의지요 결기이다

엄동설한을 이겨내고 눈 속에서 발화하는 동백꽃의 인내심
타향에서 온갖 차별과 편견을 이겨낸 디아스포라의 인내심
여러 번 죽음의 문턱을 넘기고 살아남은
말기 암 환자의 인내심은 삶을 새롭게 한다

하안거 동안거를 거친 스님들의 인내심은 무소유 무사유가
부처님께 다가갈 수 있는 빠른 길임을 깨닫는 데 있다

궂은 날씨를 참아야 하고
마누라의 잔소리를 참아야 하고
남보다 못하다는 것을 참아내야 하고
살아가기 힘든
내 삶을 참아야 한다

미혼모의 인내심 속에도
참새들의 짧은 인내심 속에도
땀과 눈물

절망과 기다림
꿈이 배어 있다

당신의 인내심 때문에
내가 자유스러울 수 있었고
당신을 사랑할 수 있었다

Endurance

Youth that staggers,

Old age that crumbles—

To live is to endure.

Endurance is not a choice,

But the will to survive,

The grit that keeps us moving forward.

The camellia,

Bursting through snow after a harsh winter—

The diaspora,

Surviving prejudice and exile—

And the cancer patient,

Having crossed the threshold of death more than once,

Finding life anew—

Each embodies the endurance that reshapes existence.

Monks who endure long retreats,

Seasons of silence,

Realize in their stillness

That no possession or thought

Can bring them closer to Buddha—

Only through this letting go

Do they arrive swiftly.

To endure bad weather,

To endure the nagging of a spouse,

To endure the knowledge

That others surpass you—

To endure the burden of living itself.

In the endurance of single mothers,

In the fleeting patience of sparrows,

Sweat and tears are sown.

In despair and waiting,

Dreams are planted.

Because of your endurance,

I was free,

And in that freedom,

I found the space to love you.

슬픔은 그렇게 시작되더이다

쌓여가는 세월의 무게로
사랑의 아픔으로
이별의 두려움으로
동행자의 무관심으로
슬픔은 그렇게 시작되더이다

모진 바람이 불어도 날아가지 않고
눈비가 내려도 씻기지 않고
모닥불에 집어넣어도 활활 타지 않는
끈적끈적한 사연으로 가슴에 쌓여가더이다

섭섭하다 말했어야 했는데
후회한다 말했어야 했는데
사랑한다
떠나지 못하게 했어야 했는데
마음을 열어 놓고 훌훌 털어버렸어야 했는데

비극 속에 잠겨 있는 슬픔은 서러워서 눈물 나게 하고
희극 속에 숨겨 있는 슬픔은 그리워서 눈물 나게 한다

내 마음이 이렇게 여리고 가벼운 줄 몰랐었다
삶에 지쳐 감정이 메말라 있을 때

애련에 물들고 후회가 쌓여가니
슬픔은 그렇게 시작되더이다

How Sadness Begins

From the weight of passing years,

From the ache of love,

From the fear of parting,

From the indifference of companions—

Thus, sadness begins.

Though fierce winds may blow,

It refuses to take flight.

Though rain may wash over,

It clings and does not wash away.

Even when cast into the fire,

It does not burn,

This sticky story gathers in the heart.

I should have spoken of my hurt,

I should have uttered my regrets,

Should have declared my love

To keep you from leaving.

Yet, I opened my heart

And cast it aside like dust.

The sadness submerged in tragedy

Brings forth tears of sorrow,
While the sadness hidden in comedy
Calls forth tears of longing.

I did not know my heart
Could be so delicate, so light.
In weariness, as emotions dried up,
I find myself tinged with sorrow,
And regret piles high.
Thus, sadness begins.

| 최윤근 |

1946년 서울 출생. 서울의대를 졸업하고, 미국에서 인턴 레지던트 수련의 과정을 마쳤다. 2014년『시로 여는 세상』신인상으로 등단하여 시집『꿈속에서 꿈을 꾸다』『아그라로 가는 길』『넌 나를 스나비쉬하다 한다』『기억 속에 흐르는 강』『늦게 쓰여진 시』『세상에 남기고 가는 것들』외에 다수의 전문 서적을 출간하였다. 미국 병원에서 마취 통증치료 전문의로 20년간 근무하다 귀국하였으며, 1994년 차병원 통증센터 소장, 1998년 차 의과대학 교수, 2002년 외국인 무료 진료소 소장, 2015년 창원시 보건소장으로 재직했다. 2014년 대한의사협회와 보령이 제정한 보령의료봉사상과 국민추천 정부 포상 대통령상을 수상하였다.

이메일 : ykchoy777@hotmail.com

가난한 시인이 된 의사

초판 인쇄 · 2024년 12월 15일
초판 발행 · 2024년 12월 20일
지은이 · 최윤근
펴낸이 · 이선희
펴낸곳 · 한국문연
서울 서대문구 증가로 31길 39, 202호
출판등록 1988년 3월 3일 제3-188호
대표전화 302-2717 | 팩스 · 6442-6053
디지털 현대시 www.koreapoem.co.kr
이메일 koreapoem@hanmail.net

ⓒ 최윤근 2024
ISBN 978-89-6104-377-9 03810

값 18,000원